TRIPLE DEUCES

A DAY IN THE LIFE OF AN AMERICAN CORRECTIONAL WORKER

Cameron K. Lindsay

PAGE PUBLISHING, INC.
New York, NY

First originally published by Page Publishing, Inc. 2018

ISBN 978-1-64214-536-6 (Paperback)
ISBN 978-1-64214-537-3 (Digital)

Printed in the United States of America

Special thanks to Sandy Wilson, Esq.

Cover design created by Mara Wilson.

For my father, Hugh Alexander Lindsay, PhD, MD.

1926 - 2015

PREFACE

At any given time in this great nation of ours, there are approximately 1.2 million people locked up in our jails, prisons, and detention centers. While I believe that all components of the criminal justice system—the police, courts, and corrections—are in dire need of overhaul, this book focuses on the correctional aspect of the system.

Arguably, the public is the least familiar with the corrections aspect of the criminal justice system. The vast majority of the public has no clue what happens inside the fences and walls of our nation's lockups. Consequently, this book attempts to provide the reader with the realities of the profession and focuses on the typical dynamics that occur in correctional facilities and the challenges facing correctional professionals. My goal is to provide a realistic, unvarnished view of what it's really like to be within the secure confines of a correctional facility.

I worked in the field of corrections for twenty-five years as a "practitioner" and currently serve as an expert witness in corrections. The views in this book are based on my personal experiences, as well as the shared experiences of other individuals whom I have had the distinct pleasure of serving with throughout my career.

While I firmly believe that our nation's criminal justice system is the best there is, unquestionably it has numerous faults, and must continually be improved if we are to move forward and evolve. Of the 1.2 million individuals who are incarcerated in the United States, approximately 95 percent of them will inevitably return to their communities; therefore, I believe we must continually strive to improve the efficiency and efficacy of our nation's correctional facilities. If we fail in this endeavor, the cycle of recidivism will continue, if not increase, and continue to provide a significant drain on society.

It's been said our prisons are a microcosm of the macrocosm of society and how we treat that segment of our incarcerated population speaks volumes. I agree. Regardless of this sentiment, I have often told friends and relatives when one works inside of a correctional facility, he or she is exposed to the very worst that human beings have to offer. While there are many positive aspects of the profession, working in a correctional facility is unquestionably dangerous and uniquely challenging, as we are attempting to "correct" human behavior in a positive manner, all while meeting our overall mission to protect the community while providing a safe and productive environment for staff and inmates.

Working as a correctional worker is one of the most arduous and complicated occupations there is. The correctional worker possesses courage while utilizing uniquely effective interpersonal skills in order to complete the job successfully and return home safely every day.

I am honored to have worked with so many brave professionals.

PROLOGUE

"All radio units, triple deuces! Say again, TRIPLE DEUCES! Location, outdoor area of A Unit!"

Dozens of correctional officers and staff from virtually every department began sprinting toward the outdoor area of A Unit. By the time I arrived at the scene, approximately six African American and eight Mexican inmates were lying on or near the sidewalk, one black guy bleeding profusely from an apparent slashing-type wound to the face and a minor stab wound to the abdomen.

On the ground were assorted homemade weapons, or "shanks," as they're referred to in the world of corrections. None were "bone crushers."

Thank goodness, I thought to myself. No, these weapons were mostly "sissy shanks" or pieces of plastic, typically fashioned from a toothbrush, whereby a razor blade is attached to one end by first melting, then while the plastic is still hot and pliable, the inmate will attach the tiny sliver of razor blade found inside disposable safety razors, and hold it in place until it dries and hardens. Real razor blades are considered hard contraband and not permitted inside the facility.

Sissy shanks aren't typically designed to kill but rather to send a message of warning by causing permanent disfigurement to the face or neck. Bone crushers, on the other hand, are all together a much different and ominous thing. Bone crushers are large, flat pieces of steel, like you might find on the inside of a locker, or as part of a larger picture frame; they are designed to cause one thing: death.

The problem here was the fact that we had a serious "virus" in the facility, meaning that because there were multiple inmates of more than one race involved in an act of violence, there was a very serious issue at hand; and if we didn't quickly get to the bottom of it, we would inevitably experience carnage at some point; carnage that quite literally risked the lives of inmates and staff. Time to lockdown and figure out what the hell was going on between our black and Latino inmates.

Once our COs, or correctional officers, got all of the inmate participants handcuffed behind their backs, our medical staff triaged the injuries, ranging from the stab wounds—which really were superficial lacerations—to minor cuts, bruises, and scrapes. The wounds, particularly the ones caused by blunt trauma, would appear a lot worse than what they actually were in a few hours once swelling occurred, but overall, there were no life-threatening injuries.

"Not good, boss," the junior grade lieutenant said to me.

"Nope, not good, LT," I replied. *Fuck.*

What everybody knew but didn't say was many staff, including my executive staff and I, would be working well beyond what we had planned on that day. That was okay with the officers and other line staff because they could soak up some serious overtime, but for us salaried folks, it was just another late evening at the joint. Family plans, as so often is the case in our world, would take a backseat. This is par for the course in the operational world of corrections.

* * *

It's a difficult thing to plan one's life around the activities of a correctional facility, particularly a high security prison like the United States Penitentiary, Canaan, Pennsylvania. Nestled in the woods of Wayne County in the far upper northeast corner of The Commonwealth, the high security penitentiary was activated as a brand-new facility in March 2005. Our Latino and black "mixer" meant a total "recall," meaning that the more than 1,400 inmates would be called, via loudspeaker, to return to their respective housing units and go directly to their cells to be locked down. The entire prison would be going into lockdown status until we got to the bottom of things and removed ringleaders and agitators from the prison's general population.

"Okay, do your thing," I said to the lieutenant. Doing his "thing" meant processing what was now a crime scene, and it would be accomplished with the precision of any crime scene reconstruction conducted by the best police detectives on the street. The goal was to maintain and record every detail of the event. The culmination of such an investigation, hopefully, would lead to the criminal prosecution of one or more inmates. I turned to my associate warden, who knew precisely what to do, but was respectfully waiting out of deference for me to green light the lockdown.

"Button everything down," I said.

"Buttoning down" officially indicated to initiate the lockdown, and that decision was made because this was an *interracial* situation that involved multiple inmates. Incidents of intra-racial violence, particularly when minor in nature and not involving multiple inmates, typically don't concern correctional administrators near as much as interracial violence. But given the facts at hand, we were all but guaranteed a shit storm was gathering on the horizon.

IN THE BEGINNING

There are very few individuals that say to themselves, "Hey, I think I want a career in corrections. Yea, that sounds like a great time. Being part of the public's general stereotype that correctional workers are abusive and ignorant, plus all that violence and social isolation, combined with mediocre pay. Sounds like just the thing for me!" No. Most of us get into corrections quite by accident. When I entered the world of the United States Department of Justice's Federal Bureau of Prisons, I had been teaching at Fairmont State College; now known as Fairmont State University in Fairmont, West Virginia. Other than measly pay, I had it made at Fairmont State. I worked easy hours, taught four criminal justice courses per semester, and was in a stimulating environment of energetic students who were eager to learn what working in the "criminal justice system" was all about.

Then, one day, the Federal Bureau of Prisons was on a recruiting trip. Fairmont State's Criminal Justice program was really coming into its own then, and while it is a relatively small college, we had about 350 criminal justice majors at the time. So the bureau visited our campus to entice some of these idealistic youngsters to federal service. As I sat in the back of the auditorium and listened to the warden of the Federal Correctional Institution, Morgantown, West Virginia, and the regional director of the agency's Northeast Regional Office, talk about career opportunities in the Bureau of Prisons, I was thinking how I couldn't wait to get out of there and get up to the campus gymnasium to engage in some three-on-three basketball.

The regional director, in his perfectly tailored suit, began talking about the salary structure of federal law enforcement positions within the Department of Justice. That garnered my attention. Bottom-line, if I entered into service at the GS-9 level, which I was sure I could qualify at, I'd be making about four grand more a year than what I was making at Fairmont. More important was the opportunity for advancement. And when the warden told us what his annual salary was, I was eager to learn more. After the meeting, I spoke with our visitors. As they were about to depart from the campus, the RD turned to the warden and said, "I want you to get this guy into an internship at Morgantown. Let's see if we can't convince him to join the bureau on a permanent basis."

That was it. That was the beginning of a twenty-five-year career in the more-than-interesting world of corrections for me, and as they say, the rest is history.

* * *

Chances are more than decent that at some time or another the proverbial excrement will hit the oscillating cooling device in every correctional facility that is of a greater security level than that of minimum or low. It *will* happen; it's simply a matter of when and why. Even the best-managed correctional facilities have issues, and the simple fact remains that human beings are resistant to having their freedom deprived or restricted. When bad things happen in correctional facilities, it is absolutely imperative that staff have well thought-out methods for responding to and controlling the situation. All correctional agencies have various methods for notifying its staff of an emergency situation. In the Federal Bureau of Prisons, there are four primary methods whereby any staff member can communicate to other staff members that things are unraveling—or about to unravel—and indicate to every employee in the facility that there is a serious issue at hand.

The first is a simple verbal radio transmission from a staff member to other radio units and the Control Center requesting assistance.

The second is a "no-dial." A no-dial is when a telephone receiver is knocked off its cradle. After a few seconds, if a staff member—or inmate for that matter—removes a phone receiver and fails to dial a number, that extended dial tone alerts into the Control Center, which is the nerve center and main communications hub in every correctional facility.

Control Center officers will note that they have a no-dial and quickly dispatch officers by radio communication to the location of the telephone showing the no-dial. So if a staff member suddenly finds his or herself in a violent situation with an inmate, or inmates, and can't get to their radio to call for help, if they can at least dislodge a receiver from its cradle, help will be on the way within minutes.

The third way to summon assistance in an emergency situation is by activating one's body alarm. There are times when a staff member is suddenly confronted with violence or a dangerous situation where they simply don't have time or an opportunity to make a verbal transmission over their two-way radio. However, if they can push a button on their radio that will activate their body alarm, and again, staff assistance will be on the way within minutes, if not sooner.

Lastly, and what is often considered to be the most urgent of all calls for assistance in all Bureau of Prisons facilities is "triple deuces." If a staff member dials "222"—triple deuces—on any phone, in any of its approximate 130 correctional facilities, Control Center officers will, as with the three other methods, send the cavalry. Inadvertent no-dials and accidental body alarm activations are not uncommon, but triple deuces is, so when that radio transmission comes over the air that a triple deuces is in effect, one's anal sphincter constricts at least a tad.

* * *

The fact of the matter is, prison and jail staff witness the very worst that human beings have to offer. Especially in high security environments where nearly all inmates have the propensity for violence and are serving life—or near life—sentences, you see very ugly things. I had served as a police officer for a few years prior to beginning my career in corrections, so I therefore felt I was already equipped to deal with the things that I would eventually see over the course of my career. In reality, however, it just doesn't work that way.

The aura of a correctional facility is an intangible thing that you have to see, hear, smell, and *feel* before it can truly be understood. And the first time those big steel doors slam behind you on the way into a facility, it gets your attention. As time goes on and one becomes a seasoned correctional worker, he or she develops a feel for the atmosphere simply by walking the facility. What you're looking for is whether inmates are interacting with other inmates and if inmates are interacting with staff. When those two things are not occurring, it invariably indicates that trouble is brewing and you had better determine what is going on before things get ugly.

The Federal Correctional Institution, Morgantown, or "Kennedy Center," as it is informally known to the locals, was not much of an introduction into the world of hardcore inmate behavior. Nevertheless, it was an important first step into the world of corrections, as I became familiar with the history and culture of the Federal Bureau of Prisons. I learned that perhaps the most important issue in any correctional facility is *respect*. Peace in a correctional facility, especially in high security level facilities, can easily be shattered when respect for others is perceived as being violated. Even seemingly simple gestures, such as cutting line in the chow hall, can quickly lead to the violator being stabbed in the neck. Why? Because it's disrespectful to do so and will absolutely not be tolerated in that environment. It is essential in a correctional environment for inmates to respect other inmates and for staff and inmates to respect each other.

I learned that new inmates are "fish," and correctional officers are bulls, hacks, "po-lice," screws, CO, the man, or guard. Frankly, all correctional officers hate being referred to as a guard. And with good reason, I believe. To escort an inmate on a hospital trip, for example, staff are literally "guarding" the inmate, so I get where the term comes from. But in the dynamic and complicated environment of a correctional facility, staff are unarmed inside the secure perimeter of the facility; therefore, it is *imperative* that they utilize the most important tool in their tool bag, that of the ability to communicate, exercise interpersonal skills, and otherwise gain the respect of convicted felons, who oftentimes have a propensity to engage in violence. Until this process is realized, influencing, guiding, and directing inmates will be ineffective.

With any time spent in a correctional facility, staff, and inmates both come to quickly realize that child molesters, women beaters, rapists, and informants—"snitches"—are the lowest forms of shit in existence. Inmates will say when an individual (staff or inmate) is exaggerating, fabricating, or making any claim or threat they can't follow through on, he is said to be "selling wolf tickets."

I learned that dangerous, higher security level inmates are known as wolves because of their predatorial ways, and that victims in society are referred to as sheep. Staff, particularly correctional officers and other staff who demonstrate courage in the performance of their duties, are known as sheepdogs. Sheepdogs are normally peaceful, but mess with a sheep, and that sheepdog pursues the wolf with unmatched determination and resolve.

While working at Morgantown, I discovered that the Federal Bureau of Prisons started with three penitentiaries: the first, Leavenworth, Kansas; the second, Atlanta, Georgia; and the third, McNeil Island, Washington State. The first director of the Bureau of Prisons was Sanford Bates, who was hired by President Herbert Hoover in 1929, and the formation of the agency was officially approved by Congress in 1930. While I learned the basics of corrections such as conducting inmate counts, key control, inmate accountability, contraband control, tool control, radio control, use of restraints, pat-down searches, strip searches, area searches, escorted trips of inmates outside the facility, and overall basic security of a correctional facility, the fact remained that Morgantown was primarily a minimum security level environment.

That meant that other than a fist fight here and there, violence was a rare occurrence. It further meant that other issues germane to higher security level environments like drug overdoses, frequent violence, self-imposed inmate racial segregation, and the possibility of an escape—the quintessential failure in corrections—were almost nonexistent.

One of my most valuable lessons at Morgantown revolves around one of the bureau's most basic management tenets, and that is *all* staff—regardless of title—are first and foremost, correctional workers. In many correctional agencies, most notably the majority of the fifty state department of corrections, so-called professional staff work in correctional facilities in a variety of positions (case workers, physicians, food service, etc.), but when the shit hits the fan and acts of violence occur, they politely remain out of the way and let the uniformed staff of correctional services respond to and handle these situations accordingly. Not so in the Bureau of Prisons. Because all staff are correctional workers first, all staff, regardless of position or status, in emergent situations, are expected to perform the duties of a correctional officer. It's one of the things that makes the bureau so different when compared to other correctional agencies in America.

* * *

Up until that point, my background had been law enforcement related, and it was abundantly clear that I knew virtually nothing about corrections, so I began to immerse myself in the history of jails, prisons, and detention centers in the United States. When analyzing our history of corrections, one can easily see that our primary philosophies have ebbed and flowed over the decades and centuries. In response to political and societal concerns—which vary quite radically depending on the specific time frame in question—one comes to realize our focus can be on retribution, incapacitation, or rehabilitation. All three categories are designed to punish and deter individuals who committed offenses deemed unacceptable by society at large. Naturally, much of our justice system was adopted from England's manner of dealing with crime, but things began to change in the late 1700s. In fact, John Howard, a Brit, wrote in 1777 that prisons should be humanized to a large degree with the focus being on penitence of the inmate, meaning that the accused should focus on his or her crime, thinking about their sins, and becoming better individuals. Howard referred to the structures that incarcerated prisoners as "penitentiaries," from the word, penitent. His ideas were largely based on the Quakers manner of reflecting on their wrongdoings.

In 1790, what is considered the first true jail in America, the Walnut Street Jail in Philadelphia, was created, and designed to incarcerate hard-core criminals. Later, in the early 1800s, the Eastern Penitentiary, near Philadelphia, and the Western Penitentiary, near Pittsburgh, were established. Inmates were to sit isolated in their cells with nothing more than a Bible and were forced to silently think about their crimes and, eventually, demonstrate a change in heart. Those who did not toe the line were flogged. Around the mid-1800s, considered the Progressive Era in US corrections history, we saw a number of new ideas emerge, such as the use of probation and parole and indeterminate prison sentences. Around 1970, our nation experienced an explosion in growth within the field of corrections as a multitude of prisons and jails were constructed and filled throughout the nation. Then, in September 1971, the world of corrections in the United States changed forever with the events that unfolded at the New York State prison called Attica. Most everybody has heard of Attica, but probably like most folks, I didn't know anything about the details of the riot in terms of how and why it occurred and how it radically changed the face of corrections in this country forever.

At the time, Attica was a racially charged environment, as more than 50 percent of the inmate population was black with the vast majority of the staff being white. Plus, the facility was severely overcrowded. The details of how and why the riot occurred are fascinating, and I highly recommend to anyone interested in American corrections to read about them. The Attica prison riot resulted in thirty-three inmate deaths, and ten staff deaths, nine of which were shot by state troopers after the inmates forced the staff to wear prison uniforms and were mistakenly thought to be inmates. There are many lessons to be learned from Attica, but one thing that has always stood out for me as I analyze the details of that horrible chapter in corrections is the fact that when there is one race of the kept and one other race of the keeper, that will invariably lead to issues. Very early in my career, this point demonstrated to me the vast importance of having a well-trained and diverse staff in every correctional facility.

THE FEDERAL CORRECTIONAL INSTITUTION, McKEAN: LESSONS LEARNED

I remained at FCI Morgantown for the duration of my internship, which was three short months during the summer of 1989. Sometime in August, I was contacted by an associate warden at the recently constructed Federal Correctional Institution, McKean, Pennsylvania, and was told there was a case manager's position waiting for me if I was interested.

FCI McKean is located in McKean County near the small city of Bradford, and in the dead of winter is typically one of the coldest spots in the nation. The AW (associate warden) who called me said he wanted to bring me on as a permanent employee and thought it would be best that I be hired in as a case manager. He said that I qualified for the position, and it was one of the most effective routes to the warden's chair. At that time, the bureau was experiencing a growth spurt that had never been seen in its near sixty-year history. It sounded good to me.

With all the futility—and, perhaps stupidity—of the "war on drugs" in full swing, prisons, especially at the federal level, were being constructed and activated at an unprecedented rate. Because I was not a permanent employee until I arrived at McKean, there was no allowance for relocation, so my wife, Dee, and I packed up a U-haul truck, attached my rust bucket of a Ford Ranger to the back of it and headed for McKean County. My new annual salary would be a whopping $26,000. It felt like we were headed for the big time. An adventure it would most definitely prove to be.

* * *

FCI McKean began accepting inmates in the fall of 1989. McKean was designated by the bureau as a medium security level facility, but to assist in the acclimation of more than half of the three hundred staff members who were new hires, the agency decided to initially send mostly low security level inmates to us, primarily who came from FCI Danbury, Connecticut, and other low security level facilities within a few hundred miles of McKean.

We would receive bus after bus, each loaded with forty inmates. Coming off the buses, inmates would be in standard prison jumpsuits and handcuffed in the front at the waist to a "belly chain" (to restrict swinging movement of the arms) and leg irons. As inmates walked the approximate eighty yards from the bus, through the front entrance of the facility and into the Receiving and Discharge area, the clinking of all those chains and hardware made an eerie sound.

Once inmates shuffled into R&D, their restraints were removed, and they were placed in a large holding cell, typically referred to as a "bull pen." Then, one by one, the inmates were taken out of the bull pen and directed to a private area where they are met by male R&D staff members, affectionately known as the "nuts and butts" crew. These R&D staff members then proceed to have the inmates completely stripped down. This is done to ensure inmates are not concealing and, therefore, attempting to introduce contraband into the facility.

Anybody that spends some time in the R&D area of a prison or jail is sure to see a plethora of interesting things. For example, inmates, particularly those who are drug addicted serving extremely long sentences and/or accustomed to violence, will go to any lengths necessary in order to smuggle their drugs or weapons into the facility.

Also, there are relatively harmless, but no less crazy things that one sees in Receiving and Discharge. There was a gay inmate who came off the bus at McKean who was the epitome of the stereotype. He walked, talked, and proudly displayed his effeminate manner in everything he did. Other inmates simply called him "Fluffy." Subsequent to being stripped, as procedure warrants, he was told to lift his penis and testicles to ensure he wasn't concealing contraband in that area, then instructed to turn around, bend over and cough; when this is done, the staff can visually inspect the rectum of the inmate, and if contraband is present, it naturally gets pushed out far enough to be seen. When Fluffy bent over and coughed for the "nuts and butts" officers, they could see something protruding from Fluffy's ass.

It was revealed by Fluffy he had been voluntarily sodomized so frequently to cause constant anal leakage. Lovely. To deal with this issue, Fluffy would take toilet paper or paper towels, roll them over and over until he had fashioned a tight stopper of sorts, then pushed it up into his rectal cavity to seal the leakage. I thought, *So this is prison.*

* * *

During my time at FCI McKean, there was a large scale disturbance that occurred at another Bureau of Prisons facility in 1991 that quickly garnered the attention of every single agency staff member, and it caused each of us to evaluate just how dangerous a correctional environment can be.

To fully understand the context of the 1991 disturbance, however, it's important to first know about another event, which occurred at two Bureau of Prisons facilities simultaneously a few years previously.

In 1980, as the communist nation of Cuba—a mere ninety miles from south Florida—suffered yet another severe economic decline, thousands of Cuban citizens wanted to immigrate to the United States. Quite unexpectedly, Fidel Castro announced that any Cuban citizen wanting to leave could do so. As we well know, communist nations don't take too kindly to those citizens who want to bail on their home country, so Castro's announcement was a surprising deviation from his past treatment of those "wanting to leave." But old

Fidel had a plan, a nefarious plan to provoke the Uni
that was to open the doors of Cuban mental health an
facilities and kick the occupants along to their good
north. The end result was by late October, approxima
Cubans, thousands of whom had severe mental illnesses and serious
criminal histories, came to America. The term "Mariel Boatlift" was
derived from the fact that most, if not all, of the aforementioned
emigrants departed for the United States from Cuba's Mariel Harbor,
thus the terms, "Mariel Cubans" and "Mariels."

It should be noted that the majority of Cubans on the Mariel
Boatlift were decent, hardworking individuals; but given the fact
that thousands were criminals and/or with severe mental health
issues, the boatlift would have far-reaching consequences. Once the
"Marielitos" were "received" in Florida, most were placed in refugee
camps, while others were held in Federal Bureau of Prisons' facilities while awaiting deportation hearings. While the majority of these
folks were law-abiding people simply looking for a better life (Who
could blame them?), only about 2 percent of the refugees were considered serious criminals, but the fact remained that those two or
three thousand individuals were not suitable to remain in the United
States.

The bottom-line with respect to the Mariel Cubans was the
fact that the vast majority of them eventually integrated in southern
Florida, primarily in the Miami area, and became productive citizens. The aforementioned minority of Mariels, however, those with
serious criminal histories and severe mental illness, having committing criminal offenses in the United States, languished in federal
prisons—even after they had served the totality of their sentences—
awaiting deportation efforts while desperately wanting to remain in
the United States.

Many of the Mariel Cubans that I had conversations with in
later years were extremely afraid to be repatriated back to Cuba for
fear that they would be killed.

Then, rather abruptly, on November 10, 1987, the United
States Department of State announced via national media that
Castro had agreed to repatriate up to 2,500 Cuban nationals, includ-

ing those who had been on the boatlifts of 1980. The problem was the State Department, quite stupidly, made this announcement to the world without first conferring with the attorney general of the United States, who heads the United States Department of Justice, which, of course, the Federal Bureau of Prisons is a component of. The results of this move were not exactly positive, to say the least.

At this time, the vast majority of the Mariels being detained seven years after the boatlift were being held in two of the bureau's correctional facilities, the United States Penitentiary, Atlanta, Georgia; and the Federal Detention Center, Oakdale, Louisiana. Within seventy-two hours or so, Cuban detainees rioted and had taken control of the Atlanta facility. The detainees' chief demand was they not be repatriated to Cuba, for fear of what would happen to them when they got there. Again, many felt they would be executed, which they may very well have, and were intent on doing whatever they needed to do to remain in the United States. It was later revealed to me by some of these individuals that they were willing to engage in just about any criminal activity, such as assaulting a correctional officer, knowing full well it would lead to criminal prosecution and eventually more time in the United States, anything to avoid returning to the likely horrors that awaited them in Cuba. Well, the shit storm at the Atlanta penitentiary lasted for eleven days; there were over a hundred—yes, more than a hundred!—hostages, and the inmates really did a number on the facility, burning down much of it. It was one of the worst, if not the very worst, riot in the history of the Federal Bureau of Prisons.

Meanwhile, on November 21, about a thousand detainees rioted and took twenty-eight Immigration and Naturalization Service and Bureau of Prisons staff hostages at the Federal Detention Center at Oakdale. The old INS, reconfigured as the US Immigration and Customs Enforcement (ICE) subsequent to "911," had a number of employees working at the federal lockup in Oakdale given the mission of that facility. In short, the Bureau of Prisons had simultaneous shit storms on their hands in Atlanta and Oakdale, and both were getting extremely ugly.

As rioting intensified at the Atlanta penitentiary, bureau officials were absolutely alarmed when they received word that inmate Thomas Silverstein had been liberated from his cell by the rioting inmates. Silverstein was a leader, if not *the* leader of the violent white supremacist prison gang, the Aryan Brotherhood.

In 1980, after becoming affiliated with the "ABs," Silverstein murdered an inmate at the United States Penitentiary in Leavenworth, Kansas, because the inmate refused to "mule" drugs throughout the facility for Silverstein and the ABs. Subsequent to his conviction, he was transferred to the United States Penitentiary, Marion, Illinois. While being housed at Marion in October 1983 in the facility's control unit, Silverstein brutally murdered Correctional Officer Meryl Clutts. Silverstein was therefore transferred to the Atlanta penitentiary where he remained until the 1987 riot. Due to the fact that the wheels had essentially come completely off in Atlanta, this particular inmate was out of his cell and on the loose throughout the facility during the initial days of the riot. Obviously, with good reason, this scared the hell out of the Bureau of Prisons leadership, and more than anything, they first wanted him back under control and in their custody.

Naturally, as a component of responding to the riot, armed staff were directed to ring the facility's perimeter to ensure an escape could not be facilitated. So, while none of the inmates were a threat to the community, as there was no way to escape, the primary concern was getting Silverstein, who had killed Officer Clutts, out of the mix and back in secure custody. This proved to be a very valid concern indeed, as it was learned during the after-action investigation subsequent to the riot that Silverstein was very much on the loose throughout the facility and was encouraging rioting inmates to kill as many of the staff hostages as possible. As negotiators established contact and communicated with the detainees, the bureau's leadership requested that Silverstein somehow be subdued and turned over to Bureau of Prisons staff.

What occurred next, at least from my perspective, was quite shocking and demonstrated an act of good faith on the part of the detainees. Subsequent to securing narcotics from the breached pharmacy within the medical unit of the penitentiary, inmates drugged Silverstein without his knowledge, and once incapacitated, the inmates "delivered" an unconscious Thomas Silverstein to bureau authorities. That's not something you see every day in the world of corrections, but it happened during negotiations before the conflict was resolved, and on December 4, 1987, the inmates voted to surrender to authorities and all hostages were released. By the time the facility was brought back under control at USP Atlanta on December 4, one inmate had been killed in the melee; and while no staff hostages were killed, some were seriously abused, physically, sexually, and emotionally. On November 29, 1987, the Cuban hostage takers at Oakdale released all hostages and agreed to end their siege by signing a document revolving around speedy review of the inmates' deportation status, improved medical treatment, and promise from the government not to retaliate against the rioting inmates. That week in November 1987 proved to be one of the most difficult in the history of the Bureau of Prisons, and set the stage for the event that occurred in 1991.

* * *

On August 21, 1991, at the Federal Correctional Institution, Talledega, Alabama, 121 Cuban inmates—the vast majority of whom had been locked up since the 1980 boatlift—rioted and took over a housing unit. It had been learned by the inmate detainees that their deportation to Cuba had been scheduled, and in short order, they would be back on Cuba's shore and, therefore, subject to whatever crazy Castro had in store for them. Things kicked off in A Unit when staff responded to a body alarm, and chaos quickly ensued when it was apparent the inmates had overpowered staff and taken their keys. Once the housing unit keys were compromised and in possession of the inmates, they began racking out other inmates who were locked in their cells. As the B-side of A Unit quickly came under complete control of the inmates, many staff were able to escape, but eleven INS and BOP staff members attempted to barricade themselves in a room. Once rioting inmates located these staff, one of the hostages was severely beaten and quickly released while another hostage, a female secretary, was released after falling ill. Ultimately, nine staff—two women and seven men—remained hostages as a protracted standoff began.

At the time the riot was unfolding, the facility's Special Operations Response Team (SORT) was engaged in training on the grounds. Once inside the facility, SORT and other staff members "belly chained" the outer unit's doors to contain the inmates and prevent the riot from spreading. Control center officers simultaneously announced a recall of all inmates in an attempt to get the remainder of the facility locked down while all female employees were removed from the facility. As a sidenote, the removal of female staff from inside an unstable correctional facility would never occur in today's Bureau of Prisons.

Special Operations Response Teams from across the bureau, as well as the Federal Bureau of Investigation's Hostage Rescue Team (HRT), were rapidly deployed to Talladega. SORT teams created an armed ring around the facility by working in shifts, all the time sitting on milk crates and monitoring any movement from within the facility.

Special trained hostage negotiators worked feverishly for ten days in an attempt to free the hostages and convince the inmates to surrender, but this proved pointless. Eventually, BOP and FBI shot callers felt the situation was deteriorating, and fearing that harm to the hostages was imminent, it was recommended to then-acting United States Attorney General William Barr that a dynamic tactical entry be executed by the FBI's Hostage Rescue Team.

Mr. Barr approved the decision, and at 3:43 a.m., the FBI's HRT stormed the unit utilizing less-lethal munitions, including stun grenades, known as "flash bangs." The entry was textbook perfect—lasting about three minutes—as the hostage takers were completely surprised, and thanks to the FBI, all hostages were freed and no inmates killed or seriously injured. In the aftermath, it was learned that the decision to storm the unit was a damn good one, as it was revealed the inmate hostage takers had forced all staff hostages to place their identification cards in a pillowcase. The reason? To decide which hostage would be murdered first in order to send a very clear message that the inmates were not fooling around as they had done in Atlanta and Oakdale four years earlier. In fact, the hostage to be killed had already been identified by the inmates, and some inmates, just prior to the decision to storm the unit, were communicating by hand signals with staff that time was getting very short for the hostages. Although I had no involvement in the Talladega hostage situation of 1991, it was an event that stayed with me throughout my career and served as a lesson of just how bad things can get inside a correctional facility. It was a stark reminder: Correctional facilities are always potentially dangerous places, and in terms of the folks who work in them, they are not for the faint-hearted.

* * *

I have always been extremely proud of how the Federal Bureau of Prisons managed their facilities, and by my own admission of bias, I believe wholeheartedly the bureau is the best correctional agency in the world. But as the saying in corrections goes, "Bad shit happens in good prisons."

Most folks, similar to that of the media, use the terms *prison* and *jail* interchangeably. The fact is they're similar, yet different animals.

Jails, most people are led to believe, house nothing more than those picked up for driving under the influence, shoplifting, and a host of other misdemeanors. When considering prisons, conversely, it is widely believed they house nothing more than a bunch of savage killers. It's a bit more complicated than that.

A jail is the initial correctional facility that a defendant enters coming off the street. Jails house inmates of every kind. In terms of *sentenced* prisoners, jails house almost exclusively those convicted of misdemeanors serious enough to warrant some form of incarceration or felonies whereby very short sentences have been imposed.

Sentenced inmates typically comprise a tiny segment of a jail's population, usually those who are serving less than one year because the vast majority of its residents are pretrial or presentenced inmates. In short, jails essentially serve to house individuals on a temporary basis until their criminal case is adjudicated. Subsequent to trial, or a plea of guilt, sentencing follows. Then the individual is designated by the correctional system to be transferred to prison for the period of their incarceration, which is almost invariably greater than one year and up to life, or, in rare cases, include the death penalty. Jails house, at least on a shorter-term basis than prisons, inmates of every kind. Yes, those charged with DUI, shoplifters, and the sundry list of other misdemeanors, but felons as well, who typically haven't been to trial and/or received their sentence yet.

In my opinion, prisons typically encounter violence of a more serious nature than jails. While there are many acts of violence, especially fistfights and assaults on inmates and staff, the majority of jail violence, at least in my experience, is without weapons. That's because inmates are transferred relatively quickly and are confined to their cells more so than in a typical prison, thus negating the need or time necessary to obtain and fashion homemade weapons.

There are exceptions to this general rule, and make no mistake, jails are *no less* dangerous than prisons; they're just different is some respects. I would say violence occurs with greater frequency in jails, but prison violence is often times not only more violent, but also better thought-out and planned and involves weapons.

Jails, especially larger ones, are extremely fast-paced environments. There are inmates coming in and going out of the facility on a constant basis. There's much more turnover in jails than prisons, so staff are exposed to different inmates and issues, even on a daily basis. It was not uncommon in large jails to process ten thousand inmates in and ten thousand inmates out, per year. What this means is that staff encounter inmates of all kind; also, because these people are typically coming right off the street, you deal not only with the addicted and withdrawing types, but those who are severely mentally ill and, more often than not, have not been treated and/or medicated for serious mental illness like outright paranoid schizophrenia.

Prisons, on the other hand, are places where staff and inmates can be in the same environment for, quite literally, many years. Prisons typically house only convicted felons, not those convicted of misdemeanors, and because an inmate of a prison—versus a jail—

will potentially be there for years to come, the acclimation to that environment is much different.

Years ago, I was speaking with a hard-core inmate who had been isolated in the prison's Special Housing Unit at the Federal Correctional Institution, McKean, due to a positive random urine test for heroin. He was African American and had been "down" (incarcerated) for, quite literally, decades. Most of his time being locked up was in high security level facilities (like Lewisburg) where he had been for about ten years just prior to being reclassified and transferred to McKean. In terms of being incarcerated in hardcore environments, this guy had been there and done that. We were chatting about high security environments, and because I had not worked in a penitentiary up to that point, I asked him what it was like, especially for weaker inmates. He said, "Lindsay…there's one of two ways in the pen…you either shit on the dick or bleed on the blade."

Huh? What the hell does that mean? is what I thought.

Sensing my ignorance, the inmate explained that in the world of high security prisons, weaker inmates become the claimed "bitch" of a strong, predatory inmate; thus, that weaker inmate now "shits on the dick" or performs sex acts at the pleasure of the predator in exchange for protection from all the other inmates who would otherwise punk him out. Conversely, had the weaker inmate refused the "protection" of the predator, he would be assaulted, if not killed, thus "bleeding on the blade."

* * *

The Federal Correctional Institution, McKean, was my real introduction to the world of corrections. Although it was classified as a medium security level facility, you see things that undoubtedly you'll see in a high security level penitentiary, but usually to a much lesser degree in terms of frequency and intensity.

When I was a unit manager at McKean, I had an inmate in my housing unit (which was one of four general housing units). He was a very dangerous individual, who because of continuing acts of violence and aggression, eventually had his security and custody levels increased and was sent to the United States Penitentiary, Marion, Illinois, which was the bureau's "supermax" facility at that time.

Unrelated to the crimes that eventually landed him in prison, this guy, according to the pre-sentence investigation (PSI) report conducted by the US Probation Officer who authored it, was in the living room of where he lived at the time, and a US Postal Service letter carrier was delivering mail to this house. The curtains, according to the letter carrier, were wide open, and he couldn't help but see inside. There he witnessed this dude sodomizing a dog. I mean, who does that? And how does that individual get to that juncture to engage in such an act?

* * *

FCI McKean was a very well managed facility where I was properly introduced to the right way of operating correctional facilities. Among many things I learned at McKean was the fact that inmates are there *as* punishment, not *for* punishment. It's a simple concept, but I had to really let that sink in. The inmate's punishment, subsequent to the court imposing sentence, is to have his/her freedom deprived; this is accomplished through incarceration. Inmates, however, do not have their freedom deprived only to be further punished at the hands of staff. It doesn't work that way, and until a staff member realizes and accepts that notion, the job of the correctional administrator is going to be inherently difficult because inmates are always going to feel and express that staff are screwing with them. And more than likely, that particular staff member will never make it in that world. Although it was a well-run facility, I saw all kinds of things at McKean that I knew existed or occurred in correctional facilities but hadn't witnessed up until that point. For example, during my first weekly tour as the facility's institution duty officer (IDO), which is assigned to all department heads to serve "as the eyes and ears of the warden in his or her absence" approximately twice a year, I walked into the inmate Visiting Room.

Being assigned as the IDO was burdensome for most department heads; it became routine for most, and because its schedule entailed hours on all shifts including weekends, it was not a coveted role.

Not the case for me though. Hell, I couldn't wait to be the duty officer. I found it exciting to patrol all over the facility, talking to staff and inmates about what was on their minds.

As I made my way through the crowded Visiting Room, I could see that the three correctional officers assigned to that post were extremely busy.

One was checking video monitors and handling paperwork; one was escorting visitors in and out of the VR and conducting nuts and butts duties due to the policy requirement that mandate all inmates be strip-searched coming into and leaving the Visiting Room; and the last officer was patrolling the area but was distracted (perhaps by design) by questions from inmates and their visitors. Off to my right, I witnessed an inmate—a guy I recognized from my unit who, according to his PSI, was a preacher on the street—standing directly behind his female visitor, who appeared to be picking something up from the floor. The inmate and his visitor had her two small children, perhaps six and eight years old, standing on either side of them, almost giving the impression that the four were embraced in some kind of odd family hug.

As I got closer, however, it became obvious that this guy was having intercourse; yes, full-blown sexual intercourse with his visitor in a room full of inmates and their visitors, including many children.

The inmate's visitor had entered the facility with no underwear and a dress that she could discreetly hike up while he unzipped his fly. They were using the children as shields. It's always amazed me what inmates thought they could get away with in Visiting Rooms and, frankly, sometimes did. Now, due to his stupidity, the inmate in question would have his visiting privileges suspended for many months.

Most people in free society think inmate visiting is what you see on TV; you know, with the ominous-looking Plexiglas that separates inmate and visitor, whereby the two never come into physical contact with each other. There are prisons, mainly supermax facilities, where staff can adequately state to the courts there exists untenable circumstances that demonstrate the inmate *must* be isolated from the outside world to include his visitors. This is very much the exception rather than the rule, however. In facilities of all security levels, contact visiting is permitted, practiced, and encouraged by prison officials, if not mandated by the courts. Noncontact visiting, with the Plexiglas and all, is very rare, and I would argue that, at least in the vast majority of situations, contact visiting is an effective management tool—one of the best, in fact.

Contact visiting, it is argued, assists the inmate, especially the inmate serving an extraordinarily lengthy sentence, to maintain physical and psychological contact with family and friends and, more indirectly, with the outside world of freedom. In short, it's one of the best management tools at the disposal of administrators. In general, I agree with this notion, but it doesn't come without problems. Some, but certainly not most, inmates will take advantage of their visiting privileges for less than altruistic purposes. Most, but not all, contraband, drugs in particular, are introduced into a correctional facility via the Visiting Room. How it normally happens is an inmate will have a well thought-out plan, which entails his visitor sneaking the drugs into the institution, typically by having the visitor wrap the drugs in small balloons then concealing it in their vagina. Male visitors, in most circumstances, hide contraband under their scrotal sack or in their rectal cavity.

Once the visitor is identified, validated as an approved visitor on the inmate's visiting list, "wanded" by a handheld metal detector, walked through metal detector, patted down and approved to enter the facility, they are escorted into the secure perimeter, and walked to the Visiting Room, where they wait for their inmate to be called from his respective housing unit to the VR and strip-searched. When the inmate enters the VR after being strip-searched, he is permitted a hug and a "brief kiss" with his visitor and may sit in a chair opposite his visitor. The small table that is situated between the inmate and visitor is low to the floor so staff can more easily recognize when the inmate and/or visitor bend down, most likely in an attempt to pass an item of contraband.

At some point during the visit, the visitor will excuse their self to go to the restroom, which, obviously, staff must permit. Once in the bathroom, in the case of a female visitor, the balloons are typically extracted from their vagina or rectum—that's a personal choice, of course—then (hopefully) after "cleaning" the balloons will place them in their mouths, most commonly under the tongue, and then reenter the VR. Shortly after the visitor rejoins the inmate he or she is visiting, the contraband is transferred from visitor to inmate either through a quick kiss, or by surreptitiously spitting the balloons into the inmate's soda or water or passed hand-to-hand.

If the balloons weren't passed during a kiss with his visitor and the cup method is chosen, then the inmate will pick up the same cup, attempting to give the nonchalant appearance of simply taking a drink.

The balloons are passed into his mouth, swallowed, and *violà!* The balloons will be passed by the inmate and ready for distribution and use within a few short days.

Years later, after my retirement from the bureau and while I was the warden of a large county jail near Philadelphia, it wasn't uncommon to have severely addicted inmates come into the R&D area and, when being stripped out, have tightly wrapped small balloons of heroin fall out of their asses. Many of these addicts, most of whom were addicted to opioids, would quickly pick the balloons up off of the floor, stuff them into their mouths, and swallow them before staff could retrieve them. Addiction is truly a state of desperation.

It's necessary to place inmates who are suspected of having contraband—typically drugs—inside their bodies on "dry cell status," meaning they are isolated in a single cell with no running water—thus, dry—and remain there until medical personnel determine that the inmate had a sufficient number of bowel movements so all of the balloons have passed through his system. Of course, some unfortunate correctional officer must pick through the excrement of the inmate with a simple wooden tongue depressor, ensuring that all contraband is identified and collected. It's a most disgusting but necessary component of managing contraband within a correctional facility.

* * *

I worked at FCI McKean for nearly eight years. By far, it was the lengthiest assignment of my career. During my tenure as unit manager, which is the individual in charge of one of the four units that houses around 250 inmates each, an inmate working in the position of "orderly" (janitor) approached me. Unless precluded due to a medical condition, all inmates in the federal system must have a job within the facility. Orderlies are responsible for performing basic janitorial services, and this particular inmate, a Mexican, took great pride in his work assignment, which was cleaning the common-area showers.

"Meester Linzee," he said, as he approached me, "Some *motherfucker* took a sheet in da shower. I kill thees man," he continued. After working through his broken English, I realized that he was telling me an inmate had taken a dump right in the shower. Accompanied by the inmate, I proceeded to walk from my office to the showers and, yep, sure enough, an inmate had taken a dump right in the damn shower.

"Okay, well, go ahead and clean it up and hopefully we'll figure out who did this," I said to the Mexican orderly. At that time, I ignorantly reasoned an inmate had defecated in the shower as a sign of disrespect, either toward staff, Mexican inmates in general, or the inmate orderly specifically. The real reason, however, was whoever had done this was simply retrieving their contraband balloons, which had been swallowed within the last day or two. It's much simpler for an inmate to retrieve balloons from his own excrement in a shower drain rather than attempting to fish them out of a toilet bowl filled with water and his waste. A lesson was to be learned here: when excrement is discovered in the shower, it's a clear indication that you've more than likely got drugs on your compound.

* * *

During my time at McKean, the No Frills Act of 1995 was a bill that was proposed by Congressman Dick Zimmer that eventually became known to us as the "Zimmer Amendment." In short, there were three major components to the bill designed to make things tougher on inmates in federal prison. First, the bill banned inmates from having access to movies that were rated X, R, and NC-17. I don't think inmates ever had legitimate access to X-rated movies, but there were cable channels carrying R-rated movies that inmates had access to before Zimmer came along. These changes made sense to me, but it sure pissed a lot of inmates off because if they wanted to see a movie, they were reduced to watching P, PG, and PG-13 rated movies. "Tough shit," the general public and politicians think. Second, the Zimmer Amendment prohibited the use of electrical musical instruments in federal correctional facilities. At that time, inmates had the ability to gain access to and play electric guitars, keyboards, and a few other electrical instruments in the recreation area of most federal prisons. This also made sense to me. The third component, and most controversial, was the abolition of inmate weightlifting equipment in all federal facilities. In truth, had the bureau immediately removed all weightlifting equipment from its prisons, there would have been a widespread shit storm in the form of riots; however, the bureau's leadership was able to successfully negotiate a deal that stipulated weightlifting equipment would be removed through attrition *or* if any equipment was used in connection with an act of violence. Once a piece of weightlifting equipment became inoperable, like a cable breaking, or a bench getting broken, then it had to go. No funds could be utilized to repair equipment. It was amusing to watch inmates jury-rig various pieces of equipment to delay their inevitable removal. The political goal was to be tougher on criminals; the philosophy was if you're in prison, you shouldn't have the luxury of working out in a gym. It's an effective plug for any politician. Plus, as the argument goes, inmates shouldn't have the ability to get all muscled up, thus having a decided advantage over staff if violence were to erupt. From the outside looking in, I understand how that makes sense. In many instances, particularly at medium and high security level facilities, the inmates screwed themselves by engaging in acts of violence utilizing weightlifting equipment. If there was a fight in the gym and one inmate hit another inmate with a dumbbell or barbell, the facility would be locked down, and every piece of weightlifting equipment was gone by the next day. At most higher security level facilities, however, inmates went to great lengths to ensure beefs among each other were handled anywhere but on or near the weight pile. There are many corrections staff who will disagree with me, but from a prison administrator's standpoint, having an inmate weight pile made good sense to me. Not to say it's never occurred, but in my career, I had no experiences with having to subject my staff to subduing a muscled-up inmate intent on engaging in violence against my staff. On the contrary, my experience is inmates who are well "vented" through the use of weight training, are typically more favorably balanced, psychologically, and less apt to act out in a negative manner toward staff. I can't tell you how many times I was warmly received by inmates whenever I visited the weight pile. Then, if I were to jump on a bench and bang out a few reps with a respectable weight, the whole joint heard about it. Undoubtedly, little things of this nature aid in developing a positive relationship with the inmate population, which can be very valuable at times when things are not going as well.

* * *

Security and custody levels are important to understand. In the Bureau of Prisons, security level indicates the type of facility and, as it pertains to the inmate, the type of prison that is appropriate for that individual's incarceration. In the Federal Bureau of Prisons, security level refers to the type of facility. Essentially, there are four security levels: minimum, low, medium, and high. Minimum security level facilities—Federal Prison Camps—are much different than the other security level facilities because they are small with usually no more than 350 inmates, and they are *not* secure environments. Almost all minimum security level camps serve as a satellite to a larger, higher security facility, located in close proximity to each other. A perfect example is that of McKean: it is a large medium security level facility, housing about 1,700 inmates while its satellite camp, FPC McKean, is located a few hundred yards from the main facility, housing around 250 inmates. Throughout my entire career, the Bureau was extremely careful with its assignments of inmates to minimum security level Federal Prison Camps.

Designated to FPCs inmates must have no violence, no escape attempts, and no history of psychological instability, outstanding warrants, or detainers, and relatively short sentences, typically not exceeding eight to ten years. Inmates assigned to camps typically have been involved in white-collar offenses like fraud, tax evasion, or low-level drug dealing, etc. In terms of political fallout and community relations, it would be nothing short of disastrous if an inmate walked into a community and committed other crimes.

Such was the case in 1987, however, when policy guidelines regarding camp placements were not nearly as stringent as they became a couple of years later, and unfortunately, the agency learned this lesson the hard way when Lynette "Squeaky" Fromme walked away from the same female minimum security level facility that Martha Stewart made famous for a short time in Alderson, West Virginia. Fromme, who had been involved with the disaster that was Charles Mansion, was charged with attempting to assassinate President Gerald Ford in 1975 and foolishly designated to FPC Alderson. She was placed in this minimum environment although she had a well-documented history of mental instability and propensity to be involved with violence.

Minimum security level facilities—known as "camps" to the feds— do not have fences, armed perimeter patrols, cells, bars, or any of the other security features one associates with a secure correctional facility. Plus, staffing to inmate ratios are much lower in a camp setting. Typically, only one correctional officer per shift is assigned in a camp setting to tend to all of the inmates, which can be as many as two or three hundred. To associate the word *honor* with inmates is incongruous, but in reality, a camp setting is largely based on the honor system. If inmates want to "walk away," which happens relatively rarely, they most certainly can, as there are no fences, alarms, and armed officers to inhibit this desire.

* * *

But each inmate in a camp knows that "walking away" is not just walking away or absconding; quite literally, the act of walking away is escaping from federal custody, and when a "camper" inmate decides to do so, he or she will be pursued by the Unites States Marshal Service, rearrested, and charged with escape. An inmate who walks away once they are back in the custody of the bureau will invariably be housed in a higher-security level facility than that of a camp. The few "walkaways" that I saw were typically preceded by a "Dear John" letter from a wife or girlfriend and doing time became too much to deal with.

Camps are almost always sleepy correctional facilities where very little happens in terms of violence and scheming on the part of its inmates. The only camp homicide in the history of the Bureau of Prisons occurred decades ago at the Federal Prison Camp, Boron, California, where one inmate killed another inmate after a disagreement. Other than the occasional fistfight, camps are laid-back environments.

Low and medium security level facilities in the Bureau of Prisons are essentially the same with respect to security features.

Low and medium facilities' perimeters include two fifteen-foot fences with multiple strands of concertina razor wire on top of, between, and around both fences. It is an ominous look to be sure.

There are "high-mast lights," at least five counts of the inmates every twenty-four hours, policy-mandated fence checks and a multitude of other security-related requirements.

Low and medium security levels facilities have at least two armed perimeter patrols at all times. Correctional officers assigned to vehicular perimeter patrol continually circle the facility perimeter in a vehicle in a slow and methodical manner, looking for any sign indicative of an escape or escape attempt. They are armed with a 12-gauge pump shotgun, an M16 submachine gun, and a nine millimeter sidearm. In terms of general security, the only difference between low and medium security level institutions is their respective staffing patterns. Both maintain essentially the same physical security features, but medium facilities are authorized a greater number of correctional staff than low security institutions. Low and medium security level facilities in the BOP are known as Federal Correctional Institutions or FCIs.

High security institutions in the bureau are referred to as USP or United States Penitentiary. Working in an USP is considered a badge of honor throughout the agency, and most staff in the agency will tell you that you really haven't been there until you've done time in a penitentiary. While the circumstances are obviously much different, it's true that staff and inmates do time together. Ironically, inmates look at that issue in the same light, in that having done time in a penitentiary is a different—yet similar—badge of honor.

Bureau USPs have all of the physical security features that FCIs have, but they also have towers, typically six to eight, on the outside of the perimeter fences that are manned by officers who are similarly armed as outside perimeter patrol officers. Some of the newer penitentiaries have an incorporated feature of a center tower, which is located smack dab in the middle of the compound or recreation area, whereby the officer is afforded a near perfect vantage point to monitor outdoor inmate activity.

In terms of institutional security levels, in addition to the aforementioned minimum, low, medium, and high security levels, there is one other: administrative. Administrative facilities in the bureau are unique because they typically house inmates of all security levels. Examples include Federal Medical Centers, which serves as a combination of federal hospital and federal prison.

Obviously, inmates of all security levels can have life-threatening ailments, so it's not unusual to have inmates of all security levels in the same administrative facility. Other hybrid BOP facilities that are designated as "administrative" include federal jails, which are known as Metropolitan Detention Centers, Metropolitan Correctional Centers, or Federal Detention Centers. Defendants are constantly coming directly from the street subsequent to arrest by federal law enforcement agencies while dozens of other inmates are headed to various court hearings, while, yet, others are being prepared for transfer to the respective facility designated for service of their sentence. Once their cases are adjudicated and the inmates are classified, you end up with a mixed bag of security levels; some will score out as minimum, yet others will be low, medium, or high security level.

Then there is the Bureau of Prisons "supermax" facility, officially designated as the United States Penitentiary, Administrative Maximum Facility (or "ADX"), Florence, Colorado. The Adminmax or ADX, as it's known among agency staff, is considered the most secure correctional facility in the county, if not the entire world. The ADX receives a fair amount of media attention and is constantly criticized for human rights issues, particularly relevant to the psychological effects of long-term isolation and the psychological treatment, or lack thereof according to its critics, afforded to inmates who are incarcerated there.

Its relatively small inmate population includes the worst of the worst or those that require special security that can't be satisfied in a normal high security level penitentiary. A typical ADX inmate has continued to demonstrate a pattern of extreme violence toward inmates and/or staff or is so notorious because of the offense history that the agency deems their placement in ADX as necessary. Inmates who are currently incarcerated at ADX, or who have done time there at some point in the past, includes quite an impressive list of America's who's who in crime to include the following:

Omar Abdel Rahman, who was convicted of seditious conspiracy for being the mastermind of the nefarious plot to blow up high-profile targets throughout New York City.

* * *

John "Jack" Powers, who was convicted of bank robbery in 1990. During the beginning phase of his incarceration, he witnessed a brutal homicide of three inmates stabbing another inmate. He was labeled a "rat" and transferred to a protective custody unit where he escaped briefly and was consequently moved to the ADX. Over the next ten years, Powers bit off two of his fingers (on different occasions), lopped off one of his testicles and mutilated his scrotum, cut off his earlobes, cut his Achilles tendon, and continued to engage in suicide attempts.

* * *

Joseph Duncan, a serial rapist and child molester, who was convicted and sentenced to death for a 2005 kidnapping and quadruple murder in Idaho.

Incidentally, the slang term for child molesters is simply "cho-mo." Cho-mos are considered the lowest form of life in the world of corrections, especially in high security environments and will be targeted for assault, or death, especially if their crimes become known to the inmate population.

* * *

Salvatore "Sammy the Bull" Gravano, the ex-underboss to Gambino Crime Family boss, John Gotti, who eventually turned government witness and whose testimony was largely responsible for the Teflon Don being sent away to federal prison until his death in 2002. By his own admission, Gravano killed at least nineteen individuals. The feds wanted Gotti so badly that Gravano was nevertheless placed in the government's federal witness security protection program. Eventually, however, he was removed from the Witness Security program. Subsequently, Gravano was living openly and providing interviews to the media until he picked up a drug distribution charge in Arizona and was returned to prison.

* * *

David Lane, a hard-core white supremacist convicted of conspiracy, racketeering, and civil rights violations in the murder of Denver Jewish "shock-jock" Alan Berg.

* * *

Ted "The Unabomber" Kaczynski, the man who had earned a PhD in mathematics and who, from 1978 until his arrest in1995, killed three and injured twenty-three people with explosive devices that he assembled and mailed to his intended victim targets.

* * *

Barry "The Baron" Mills, one of the three counsel leaders of the white supremacist group, The Aryan Brotherhood. Mills has been locked up almost continuously since 1969 and widely believed to have ordered the deaths of many individuals. He was convicted for the near-decapitation murder of an inmate in 1979.

* * *

Zacarious Moussaoui, the French native who pled guilty to conspiring to kill Americans in the September 11, 2001, attacks.

* * *

Robert Hanson, the former special agent of the Federal Bureau of Investigation turned traitor, who spied for the Soviet Union and Russian intelligence components is serving fifteen consecutive life sentences.

* * *

Nicodemo "Little Nicky" Scarfo, the former boss of the Philadelphia Bruno Crime Family, who is serving life for multiple counts of murder convictions.

* * *

Anthony "Gaspipe" Casso, the former underboss of the Lucchese Crime Family, widely known as a "homicidal maniac," had previously been placed in the Federal Witness Protection program but was subsequently removed for repeated violations.

* * *

Terry Nichols, who was part of the 1995 conspiracy, along with Timothy McVeigh, to bomb the Alfred P. Murrah Federal Building in Oklahoma City. He was sentenced to 161 life sentences.

* * *

Timothy McVeigh, the mastermind of the Oklahoma City Murrah Federal Building bombing. McVeigh was eventually moved to the United States Penitentiary, Terre Haute, Indiana, the federal government's only "death house" where he was executed by lethal injection in 2001.

* * *

The bottom-line goal with security levels is to ensure that like inmates are housed together in an atmosphere of security commensurate with the offense history of the offender. Think of it as keeping the sheep with the sheep and the wolves with the wolves in an appropriately secure correctional facility.

In terms of custody level, these are assignments given to inmates based on a quantified, objective scoring method referred to as custody classification. Every inmate in the Bureau of Prisons is assigned a custody level, which indicates the level of supervision, constraints, and type of restraints to be used on the inmate during movement inside and outside of the facility.

Inmate custody levels include community, out, in, and max. Custody levels are derived primarily from the inmate's background, level of violence, and his behavior during incarceration. Some of the many elements that are factored in the scoring process include the instant offense (which is the charge that got the inmate where he is), prior convictions, outstanding detainers and/or warrants, length of sentence, percentage of the sentence that has already been served, institutional adjustment (number of incident reports and the severity of each), family ties, psychological history, whether or not they are paying the fine(s) and meeting financial obligations, etc. So every inmate is assigned a security level, indicating the appropriate facility in terms of security level where he/she should be housed, and a custody level, indicating the degree of control the inmate must come under, and the types of restraints that policy requires when being transported anywhere outside the facility, etc.

So if I'm interested in knowing what kind of inmate I'm dealing with, a quick look at his or her file reveals a great deal of useful information. In short, I can discern if an inmate is classified as a medium/in inmate or low/out, etc. The typical security level and custody level of a camp inmate is minimum (security level)/community (custody); conversely, most inmates at medium and high security level facilities are classified as high/in or medium/in. Typically, those inmates incarcerated at the Admin Max (the BOP's "supermax") would be classified as high/max.

The interesting thing is an inmate can engage in positive institutional adjustment during their period of incarceration and "graduate" downwards on the scale. Just because an inmate is scored as a high security level with max custody today, doesn't necessarily mean he can't be a medium/in five years from now. There are some hard-and-fast rules that preclude inmates from sliding from the extreme high end of the scale to the other, such as a bank robber who killed someone in a robbery ever being assigned community custody, and thus being appropriate for camp placement. However, most inmates can make serious progress on the type of facility they are quartered in and the restrictions within that facility based on the service of time and positive institutional adjustment.

* * *

McKean, as previously mentioned, was designated as a medium security level facility, meaning that we had some serious inmates, many who had violence in their past. It certainly wasn't a penitentiary-like environment where there is a much greater degree of violence, but we certainly had our fair number of shitheads there. We had a Jamaican inmate that came to us on a transfer and, due to his well-documented history of disciplinary infractions, was housed in the Special Housing Unit. Special Housing Units (SHU) serve as the prison within the prison. Rather than enjoying the relative freedom that inmates in general population are afforded, inmates in the SHU, conversely, are locked in their cell—oftentimes with another inmate—for twenty-three hours a day. The one remaining hour is for recreation time, which is conducted in a small fenced-in area, perhaps the size of an average kitchen.

This Jamaican was a number one rated pain in the ass and constantly screwed with staff. He loved to write with his excrement, quite literally, all over the inside of his cell and cell-door window, which has to be unobscured so staff can periodically monitor the activity of the inmate. He knew that sooner or later, staff would invariably have to remove him to another area while the cell was cleaned and disinfected. The same inmate was fond of throwing "cocktails" at staff through the food tray slot when it needed to be opened. Cocktails, in corrections parlance, is the lovely combination of an inmate's feces and urine, which is combined by the unruly inmate and thrown on staff. One might assume this particular inmate was mentally ill; on the contrary, he was locked up by the feds for committing crimes in the United States, but he also was facing murder charges in his home country and knew quite possibly he faced execution if extradited. He therefore engaged in a continuous pattern of disruptive behavior, thus continuing and extending his administratively imposed stay in our Special Housing Unit, while simultaneously attempting to pick up new criminal charges. This dude was eventually extradited back to Jamaica on an aggravated murder charge, the only crime for which the death penalty may be imposed in Jamaica. Although unconfirmed, we had heard through unofficial channels that he had been executed by Jamaica, utilizing their only method for executions: by hanging.

During my time at FCI McKean, the Bureau of Prisons designated the United States Penitentiary, Terre Haute, Indiana, as the agency's new "death house," officially known as the Special Confinement Unit. This unit would serve as death row for the feds. Juan Raul Garza and Timothy McVeigh were executed there in 2001, and Louis Jones, Jr., in 2003. Today, there are about sixty inmates in Terre Haute's SCU, including the racist Charleston, South Carolina murderer, Dylann Roof.

* * *

People frequently ask me how true the stereotypes are with respect to sexual assaults in jails and prisons. That's tough to answer because it largely depends on the type of facility and how well it's managed. Make no mistake, rapes occur in correctional facilities, but I had never been exposed to it until I worked in a penitentiary setting. It happens very rarely in lower level security facilities. In terms of consensual sex acts, I've always been fascinated with the inmate who was a hardcore heterosexual in free society that turns to homosexuality in prison. Again, during my unit manager days at McKean, while assisting the correctional officer assigned to my unit in looking for an inmate missing from his work detail, we happened to glance in a cell that we were passing. Inside, one inmate was on top of another inmate in missionary fashion, except that the inmate who was being sodomized had his knees pinned back by his ears. I personally have no issues with those who are homosexual, but quite honestly, I was shocked by seeing something like that. Sure, it happens, but actually seeing something that foreign to me was a shock. The Bureau prohibits all sex acts in its facilities. Regardless if "consensual" or not, sex acts are not permitted in prison because it can easily lead to more serious issues including extortion, rape, pimping, and other forms of violence. Strange things of a sexual nature, none of which are ever good, occur in correctional facilities with a high degree of regularity. Don't ask me why it was germane to Latino inmates, but one of the weirdest things that I had come across in a correctional environment involved inmates of Latin descent, mostly Mexicans and Dominicans, attempting to gain access to rosary beads. Rosary beads were most definitely the preference of choice, but when beads of this shape and size were not accessible, domino pieces from a game set would be stolen and later broken into small pieces whereby the pieces could be filed into small bead-like shapes. The inmate would then, in most cases, have another inmate slice the foreskin of his penis lengthwise, insert the pieces, and then be crudely stitched up. The purpose of this insanity is once the inmate is back in free society and able to engage in sexual activity with his lady, the beads would provide added stimulation for her.

There were two primary problems that we encountered with this form of self-mutilation. First, there was obviously a high rate of infections and, second, in cases of an unsteady, unskilled hand, some inmates damn near had their Johnson lopped right off, and would eventually have to come to staff for medical assistance, which would require a medical trip to a hospital in the local community. Inherently this presents potential threats to staff who escort the inmate on such a trip.

Not good.

* * *

It's interesting that the public's perception, in general, is that most prison and jail employees are stupid and corrupt. And while there couldn't be anything further from the truth, the sad fact remains that a small minority of employees will fulfill this stereotype. After twenty-five years as a correctional "practitioner" and four years as an expert witness in the world of correctional litigation, I've tried my best to objectively quantify, in an empirical sense, the percentage of staff that become "dirty."

When I became a warden for the first time in 2002, and up until I retired as a warden in 2014, my executive staff and I would constantly attempt to quantify and qualify the degree of staff corruption in the respective facilities we worked in. Obviously, there are shit heads in every profession: attorneys, physicians, teachers, bakers, accountants, engineers, bankers, whatever…name any profession you like, they're there too. And while I have no reason to believe the profession of corrections is any worst in terms of the percentage of bad apples, my best estimation is approximately 1 to 2 percent of an entire prison or jail staff will be corrupt.

That may not sound too bad, but it is because this small minority of self-serving assholes risks the safety, security, and overall orderly operation of the correctional facility. To prove this point, one simply has to look at what occurred at the Clinton Correctional Facility, a maximum (high) security level facility in the New York State Department of Corrections and Community Supervision, located in the far reaches of the northern part of New York. On June 6, 2015, inmates Richard Matt and David Sweat escaped from Clinton, precipitating a manhunt of astounding proportions, which culminated approximately three weeks later when Matt was shot and killed by border patrol officers on June 26, some fifty miles from the prison. Sweat was shot twice by a New York State Trooper on June 28, about sixteen miles from where Matt had been killed and only about a mile and a half from the Canadian border.

Sweat lived and later provided information about the details of the escape that is believed to have cost the taxpayers of New York well over $20 *million* dollars. On June 7, staff discovered an external breach at the facility in that a manhole cover was open that led from the bowels of the prison. Once Matt and Sweat were deemed missing and therefore at large, prison officials were convinced the two murderers had help from corrupt staff. They were right. The investigation into the escape revealed that prison employee, Joyce Mitchell, had been compromised by both inmates and was reported to have engaged in a sexual relationship with Matt. Consequently, she allegedly provided Matt and Sweat with hacksaw blades, chisels, and other tools. Mitchell, according to the plan, was to be the getaway driver but backed out when she caught a case of conscience. Mitchell also admitted to entering into a murder conspiracy with Matt by planning to assist in the killing of her husband with the assistance of Matt, then ride off into the sunset with the convicted murder. Another prison employee, Correctional Officer Gene Palmer, admitted smuggling tools into the facility for Matt in exchange for paintings. He subsequently pled not guilty to the charges brought against him, which, if found guilty, could garner a twenty-year prison sentence.

So if my estimations are accurate, in a large facility of six hundred staff, it's conceivable that at least six and upwards of twelve staff are dirty! Talk about a management nightmare with the overall safety and security of the facility being jeopardized, not to mention the tremendous political fallout that accompanies a fiasco, like a staff member being indicted for assisting—intentionally or unintentionally—an inmate who ends up escaping.

In the federal system, as well as all state systems, it is illegal for a staff member to have any kind of sexual contact with an inmate, but I have seen staff—men and women—trash their careers and personal lives by engaging in some form of sexual activity with an inmate. In my experience, when staff engage in sex acts with an inmate, ninety-nine times out of a hundred it is voluntary on the part of the inmate; in fact, in the vast majority of cases like these, the inmate has slowly and methodically "worked" the staff member, manipulating him or her to feel comfortable enough to begin "trusting" the inmate.

Inmates have all the time in the world, so to speak, to watch the actions of staff members. From my perspective, most inmates are intelligent, cunning, shrewd, and *very* observant.

In short order, they can discern which staff are aggressive and enforce the rules to a "T," which staff are assertive—from my perspective the ones who have the most common sense and will stand up to inmates when necessary, but flexible enough to be reasonable—and which staff are passive, having a high need for approval, and will avoid confrontation in just about any form. In the world of corrections, the words *trust* and *inmate* are totally incongruous. This is one of most basic tenets of surviving as a correctional worker: *never* trust an inmate.

As a correctional professional, you have an obligation to be respectful, responsive, and professional in all of your interactions with all inmates at all times, but you *never* trust an inmate. In nearly every single one of the cases when staff trusted an inmate, the inmate was not acting out of some form of altruism or genuine care or love for the employee. Hell no. When internal prison investigators get wise to one of these situations and confront the inmate, almost invariably they will give up the staff member, claiming to be a victim. The thing is, they're right, at least by definition of the law; plus, staff members have an obligation not to cross that line.

I'm reminded of one of those one in a thousand instances when the inmate didn't blame or give the staff member up. At the Metropolitan Detention Center in Brooklyn, two years before I took over as warden, there was an attractive female psychologist working at the facility. She was a former New York City Police Department psychologist and, from all accounts, was very competent and capable. She was eventually accused of having a sexual relationship with a Bloods gang leader in New York City. It was alleged that she kept the gang member on suicide watch for the purpose of spending intimate, one-on-one time with him. While the gang member's own family said he was sweet and intelligent, they further described him as having a strong propensity toward violence and manipulation. In the end though, the inmate refused to give the psychologist up, stating the two were merely "friends." I assure you this is very much the exception to the rule. I can't tell you how many times over the course of my career when I saw a staff member fall in love—or think they had fallen in love—with an inmate. Of course, that scenario never ended well.

The following is very similar to many of the other compromising situations that staff put themselves in throughout my career. During the course of a routine search of an inmate's personal belongings, a correctional officer discovered a letter signed by what clearly appeared to be a female who happened to have the same name as the female who worked in the same housing unit where he worked and where the inmate was housed. Coincidence? Unfortunately, not. The astute officer who had conducted the search wisely turned the letter over to the Special Investigative Supervisor (SIS), who initiated an internal investigation to ensure there was no connection between the inmate, love letter, and the female officer with the same name. Every secure (low, medium, high, and administrative security level) Bureau of Prisons facility has an SIS who, essentially, is the detective-like investigator inside the facility. In this matter, the SIS retrieved the officer's personnel file from the Human Resources Department and compared the writing of the love letter with that of the officer. Dead match. Next the SIS went into the inmate telephone system and brought up all of the recent calls the inmate had made. All telephone conversations that inmates make—excluding legal calls—are recorded and maintained for a period of time for posterity purposes. On one such call, undeniably, the staff member's voice was the same as what we heard on the tape. The staff member, when confronted by the SIS, resigned on the spot. She could have been prosecuted, but in reality, in cases without aggravating circumstances, most federal prosecutors are not interested in expending the time and money to prosecute "minor" cases of staff corruption.

* * *

There's a term used in the world of corrections, POS, or piece of shit, which is admittedly used with some degree of regularity. Most certainly, not all inmates are classified by staff as POS; conversely, very few are.

And there are some staff members—a tiny minority—who are known to facility leadership and their peers alike as a POS. A POS staff member is one who compromises the safety and security of the facility by introducing contraband (weapons, drugs, alcohol, or forms of "soft contraband," like food) to be passed to inmates. Or the rare staff member who is a predator and will look for opportunities, for example, to have sex with inmates. Then there is the POS staff member who, if not outright sadistic, enjoys being in a position of power and control over inmates, thus threatening the overall safety and security of the facility.

* * *

There was one case of staff corruption that occurred many years ago, but it was downright infamous throughout the ranks of the bureau.

There are a multitude of departments in every federal correctional facility, but the backbone of every BOP facility is the Correctional Services Department. Correctional Services is typically comprised of dozens of correctional officers of four different grades (pay scales), junior lieutenants, senior lieutenants, and a captain. The captain is what was referred to in the old days as "chief of the guard." Next to the warden and associate wardens, the captain—also a member of the warden's executive staff—is a very powerful and influential individual in any federal facility. There was a facility in the bureau where the captain—a male—was discovered to have been performing fellatio on inmates within that facility's population. Staff misconduct of a sexual nature can occur among either gender with either inmate gender. I've seen all possible combinations.

Then there are those predatorial male staff who prey on their female inmate victims. While these individuals represent a tiny minority of staff overall, there's no doubt they exist and must be eradicated from the profession of corrections.

In 1997, the Federal Correctional Institution, Dublin, California, came under intense scrutiny due to alleged sexual misconduct by some of the male correctional staff. An all-female facility at the time, three Dublin inmates brought suit against the federal government due to a "pattern of and practice of sexual assaults, intimidation, physical, sexual, and verbal abuse, threats of violence, sexual harassment, invasion of privacy, and other violations of the law." The suit was eventually settled, but not before the bureau agreed to sweeping policy and procedural changes including, but not limited to, incorporating reporting procedures to inmates during admission and orientation training, staff training, and monitoring and enforcement procedures for bureau wardens.

* * *

There was a correctional counselor who worked for me who had sex with at least one inmate on a few occasions. This guy would call the inmate to a secluded area, have sex with her, and have her return to her housing unit. According to the counselor, he said the female inmate had flirted and enticed him into the situation and that he "became weak."

After this had occurred a couple of times, the inmate reported it to a first-line supervisor who, in turn, reported it up through the chain of command where it landed in my lap the following day. When I brought the counselor into my office with two of my associate wardens and our special investigative supervisor, I gave him an opportunity to resign, explaining that we would pursue termination if the allegations were sustained against him. He resigned on the spot and, as is the case most of the time, the inmate sued the government. Her case eventually settled out of court.

* * *

FCI McKean was, and is to this day, an all-male facility. In the mid-nineties, we had an inmate who was in the process of undergoing a sex change. This particular inmate had breasts that just about any woman would envy, but he hadn't got around to altering the downstairs plumbing yet and, therefore, still had a penis and testicles. The inmate went by "Brenda," and that's what other inmates and staff referred to her/him as. Needless to say, staff kept Brenda under close watch because we knew—whether he/she was interested or not—there would be a host of willing inmates attempting to take advantage of him/her.

* * *

We had an inmate who was processed into the facility and in the process of becoming transsexual. This particular individual had already acquired breasts that resembled that of a busty woman, yet still maintained a penis (downstairs "plumbing"). Inmates going through this transition are oftentimes in corrections referred to as a "he-she." This particular inmate had come into the facility wearing pumps, huge eyelashes, a hairweave, and amber-colored contact lenses. If you saw him/her on the street, you would swear you were looking at an attractive woman. Not so much, however, once all the aforementioned items were removed.

* * *

I would argue that men, in general, are violent, at least to some degree, by nature. Put a bunch of men together, involuntarily, and ask them to live in close quarters with one another, and you're guaranteed to have violence, everything from slap fights, to fistfights, and outright assaults.

It's just the way it is. Now take a thousand or two thousand men or so, all of whom have felony convictions, plus a documented history of violence. Well, it doesn't take a nuclear physicist to figure out you just may want to button your chin strap for the ride. That's what a high security environment is. Working in a high security environment is like nothing else. There will be times when you will be scared shitless; if not, then you're insane. And you will see things—the very worst that human beings have to offer—that, if you're not in tune with how to appropriately deal with it, will leave you bitter, jaded, angry, and distrustful of *all* people. It can easily affect one's personal relationships and their lives overall.

In my experience, it's interesting to note that staff get along better and work as a team of one in a penitentiary relative to a lower security facility like a federal prison camp—and to a lesser degree—a federal correctional institution, because in lower level security facilities, the frequency and severity of violence are much less compared to high security facilities. When your ass is on the line every day, people

CAMERON K. LINDSAY

have a tendency to be more focused on the task at hand rather than the petty bullshit that so much of us engage in when not.

In lower security environments, staff usually do not encounter serious danger and life-threatening situations; therefore, the level of camaraderie does not exist to the degree that one invariably finds in a penitentiary setting. The most common form of "therapy" that I witnessed was the use of alcohol. Many BOP staff, especially those at the penitentiaries, *love* to party, and since staff are drug tested on a routine basis, the (legal) drug of choice is alcohol. Talk about parties!

I think there were so many wild penitentiary parties because staff, especially in high security environments are, quite literally, dealing with their post-traumatic stress by self-medicating with booze. Hell, if you see an inmate get stabbed in the neck with blood spurting all over the place, even if the inmate lives, that kind of thing stays with you. And that's not exactly something you shoot the shit with the next-door neighbor about.

And that's just inmate-on-inmate violence. Inmate violence against staff is a whole other subject.

* * *

The murder of a staff member at the hands of an inmate is extremely rare, as there have been twenty-six staff members—the vast majority being correctional officers—who have been killed by inmates in the line of duty since the agency's formation in 1930. The incident of October 22, 1983, at the United States Penitentiary, Marion, Illinois, is something that's stuck with me since I first learned about it during my introductory training at FCI Morgantown.

Even though the incident occurred six years before I began my career, it was something I thought about frequently as I matriculated through my bureau journey, especially as I rose into the positions of associate warden and warden. When you get to that level, you feel a great deal of responsibility for the safety of your staff, the community, and yes, even the inmates themselves.

On that fateful October day at Marion, three correctional officers had entered onto a range in the Special Housing Unit of the

56

facility. One of the officers handcuffed inmate Thomas "Terrible Tom" Silverstein in the front of his body and removed him from the shower to be returned to his cell. Had Silverstein been appropriately handcuffed—behind his back—the terrible incident to follow may have been abated. Silverstein was a member of the white supremacist group, the Aryan Brotherhood, and had a raging hatred for BOP staff.

Silverstein, while being escorted, leaned down to ostensibly converse momentarily with another inmate who was locked in his cell, but his food slot was opened (another breach of security). One of the officers heard a click that sounded like handcuffs being unlocked. Unfortunately, that was precisely what he heard. The inmate in the cell lifted up his shirt whereby Silverstein, who was being escorted, could reach through the bars of the cell and take possession of a shank. Obviously, the assault had been well planned and the inmates took advantage of the security shortcuts that staff were taking in the Special Housing Unit.

The officer who witnessed this suddenly yelled that the inmate had a shank. Silverstein then quickly ran down the range and began viciously stabbing one of the correctional officers, Meryl Clutts. Officer Clutts broke away from the inmate and ran toward the front of the range, attempting to get to the door. Silverstein quickly pounced on Officer Clutts and began stabbing him more. At this point, one of the other officers hit Silverstein in the head with a riot baton, and he backed away while Officer Clutts was removed from the area. Officer Meryl Clutts was pronounced dead on arrival at the local community hospital.

The homicide of a staff member is an indescribably traumatic event, particularly on the entire staff at the institution where it occurs. The lingering multitude of feelings precipitated by such an event hang over the facility until every single staff member that was employed at the time of the homicide has retired. Then, and only then, does the healing really begin. What the staff and their families at USP Marion experienced on October 22, 1983, is beyond comprehension. Sadly, subsequent to the shockingly vicious murder of Officer Meryl Clutts at the United States Penitentiary, Marion, the facility continued to operate as normal throughout the day of October 22, even in the Special Housing Unit where Clutts had been killed just hours earlier.

Later that day, an inmate was being removed from the recreation cage in the Special Housing Unit in order to be returned to his cell. Two officers, one of which was Robert Hoffman, were conducting the move. While being escorted, the inmate, Clayton Fountain, also an Aryan Brotherhood member, walked ahead of the escorting officers, his back to the staff members, and stopped at another inmate's cell. Fountain suddenly turned toward the staff, his handcuffs defeated and a shank in hand, and began stabbing Officer Hoffman, killing him, and injuring two other officers. It was later revealed that because Fountain didn't want Silverstein to be the only AB who had murdered a staff member, Fountain killed Officer Hoffman simply to even the score.

There had never been two Bureau of Prisons staff members killed in the line of duty on the same day—let alone at the same facility—nor has there been since. The Marion incident eventually served as an agency-wide training tool in terms of the management and movement of inmates in Special Housing Units, and administrative decision-making subsequent to critical incidents occurring. After Officers Clutts and Hoffman had been murdered, USP Marion locked down and evolved into the Federal Bureau of Prison's first "supermax" facility and stayed that way for the next twenty-three years.

* * *

FCI McKean was a great learning experience that served me extremely well over the course of my entire career. It opened my eyes to what life was like inside a secure correctional facility for staff and inmates. Learning the basics of managing a correctional facility, staff/inmate interactions, inmate manipulation, the psychology and process of staff corruption, how weapons are manufactured, and all the other basics of sound safety and security of the facility—as well as the history and culture of the agency—were learned at McKean.

One summer afternoon, as our warden and two of his three associate wardens were attending a meeting in Bradford, we had an incident on the recreation yard that damn near led to a full-scale shit storm. Keep in mind this was in the mid-1990s, years before the events of 9/11 that changed the world. The backdrop of the situation is this: in those days, the seeds of radical Islam had recently been planted and were beginning to grow. Fueled by racism, socioeconomic disparity, and still suffering from the hangover of racial segregation, I would argue that the radicalization of the Muslim religion in this county has its origins in our prisons, beginning in the late 1960s and early 1970s. Whether intentional or not, as we got into the nineties and the war on drugs raged, the issue of drug law and sentence structure inequities certainly gave the impression of focusing enforcement on minority populations.

Consequently, dissent fermented in our prisons. FCI McKean was no different, and some Bureau of Prisons' ecumenical chapels served as the hotspot within facilities where radical leaders could spew their poison and attempt, with a relatively high degree of success, to "program" and motivate their protégés to action.

With those dynamics at hand on this particular summer day when, of course, the facility's leadership was approximately thirty minutes from the prison, everything seemed to quickly become unhinged. The remaining associate warden was a guy that was unaccustomed to acting in the position of warden and, from my perspective, wanted nothing to do with it. Nevertheless, he was the acting jack on that day at that time, and it was necessary to step up and deal with the situation.

There were approximately five hundred inmates on the yard, including about thirty Nation of Islam (NOI) inmates, who began to unfurl their prayer rugs right there on the yard, which of course was prohibited. This group of inmates subsequently kneeled on the prayer rugs and began to pray. This was a problem. All the other inmates could see that a relatively small group of inmates was violating the rules of the facility. Would staff intervene and take corrective action? If not, the message would be inmates can feel free to run us over anytime they damn well please. However, on the other hand, if we were to intervene—which, of course, we had to—how would it be handled? And those types of decisions have significant outcomes and consequences. The *how* part of this decision was crucial.

Before word had reached the warden's office, a young lieutenant and a recreation specialist approached the Imam, or spiritual leader, of the group and told them they needed to knock the shit off and cease to engage in the overt practice of religion in an authorized area. As an important sidenote, the lieutenant came armed with a video camera and had begun recording the interactions. Videotaping the incident was, in fact, a good idea and consistent with correctional standards; however, if the taping could not be accomplished surreptitiously, then the *first* best course of action would have simply been to approach the inmates and have a respectful, polite discussion on why their behavior was inappropriate and ask them to desist.

When a staff member *asks* an inmate to do something, it is, in essence, an order to do something. But when the circumstances allow, being polite and respectful is always the best approach in these situations; it's an effective diffusion technique. Yet, in this particular situation, we had a small group of inmates who made it abundantly clear that they hated the "blue-eyed devil," and we were about to interrupt their prayer session, all while hundreds of other inmates looked on.

In these situations, the last thing you need is a match to ignite a spark, and we were right on the edge of lighting the yard up. Engaging thirty or so inmates in a defiant situation is one thing; confronting them in front of hundreds of other inmates is quite another. When the call came into the warden's office that the shit was about to hit the fan on the yard, the AW asked me to report to the yard and attempt to assist him in resolving the situation.

In the back of every staff members' mind was if things started to come unglued, some inmates could turn on the NOI inmates, some could turn on us, some might do the right thing, or all of them could turn on us. It was a very tense situation. After the incident, I took some heat from a few correctional staff because my decision upon arriving on scene was to have the video camera taken away. That could have resulted in a bad situation and ultimately been a bad decision. Luckily, however, after the camera was removed from the scene, the NOIs began to chill, and eventually they complied with our "request" to stop praying on the rec yard. In no way am I saying my decision was the right one; it just happened to, luckily, work in that situation.

* * *

There was one incident in particular that occurred at the Federal Correctional Institution, McKean, that didn't go so well, and served as the best learning experience for me, and will remain with me life-long: October 1995.

In October of 1995, disparity in federal sentencing between crack and powder cocaine came to a head, and it was manifested by the actions of inmates at dozens of facilities throughout the Federal Bureau of Prisons.

Cocaine use was in full swing in the nineties, and with the ongoing "war on drugs," individuals were being locked up at an unprecedented rate. Prisons couldn't be built fast enough to house all of the people being sentenced. In short, we as staff were caught in the middle of a political nightmare that was beginning to manifest in federal prisons throughout the country.

At that time, the federal sentencing guidelines were astronomically higher for cocaine in crack form in comparison to cocaine in powder form, and congress had thus far refused to negate the gross disparity between the two. The issue was much deeper, however, in that the drug of choice for largely inner-city, thus, mostly people of color, was crack, while the drug of choice for affluent suburbanites, thus mostly white people, was powder cocaine. Consequently, this became, quite naturally, a racially fueled issue. Between October 19 and October 26, the shit hit the fan at dozens of federal facilities nationwide. Our day in the box was October 24, 1995.

I had gone home from work on October 23 knowing that we very well could have a problem at our facility the next morning. The intelligence we had developed thus far indicated we would more than likely have a small-scale work strike, meaning inmates would make a point by refusing to report to their job assignments. I was the administrative duty officer that week, so we had planned in advance that if the first group of inmates who were called for work refused to report, I would come to the facility and get the ball rolling with respect to getting executive staff notified and initiate staff recall.

The first group of inmates called for work detail in federal prisons is the kitchen inmates, who are called at 4:00 a.m. every morning to begin preparing the morning meal for the entire inmate population. As anticipated, I received a call from our control center officers notifying me the kitchen detail had refused to report for work. Later we learned that most of these inmates wanted to work but were in fear of being retaliated against by other inmates if they didn't demonstrate solidarity by refusing to work.

I arrived at the facility at about 4:30 a.m. and went directly to the warden's office where I was met by another member of the warden's executive staff, the camp administrator, who was the highest-ranking member at the facility at that time. As a precautionary measure, he had already ordered all correctional officers into the sally ports, a secure foyer-like vestibule between the main front door of each housing unit and the interior door leading into the common area of the unit where the inmates' cells were. I had convinced him that because I had a good rapport with the inmates, I should go into the housing unit and attempt to reason with the inmate ringleaders of what appeared to be a work or food strike. With great reluctance, he agreed.

As I made the approximate one hundred yard walk from the administration building to Unit 2, I could see the correctional officer on the "A" side of the unit inside the sally port, observing what was occurring inside the unit. When I arrived, I told him to unlock the door and allow me to enter. He looked at me like I was nuts and asked if I was sure. I said I was, so he opened the door and relocked it as I entered.

When I entered the unit, it was eerily quiet and dimly lit. Foolishly, I sauntered farther into the unit and walked up the stairs to the second floor, which serves as the top range of one side of the bow-tie-shaped housing unit. The moment I got onto the landing of the second floor, I was shocked to see that all inmates had come out of their cells—which were not equipped with automated locks in those days—and were standing in front of their respective cells, wearing hoods over their faces.

Oh, shit, I thought. Trying to steady my voice, I asked the inmates what the problem was and if there was any way we could peacefully resolve the situation before things got out of control. Not one inmate said one word. They simply stared at me. I felt a chill down my spine and a sickening feeling in my gut. I nervously turned around and tried to casually walk back down the stairs where the correctional officer quickly let me out of the unit and relocked the sally port door.

As the day progressed and we learned through their actions just how serious the inmates were, it dawned on me just how stupid my decision was to go into that unit. It proved to be the dumbest thing I had ever done in my career, and I was very fortunate to not have been assaulted and/or taken hostage.

By mid-morning, our Special Operations Response Team—trained and equipped like a traditional police Special Weapons and Assault Team (SWAT)—Disturbance Control Teams, and other staff had quelled what was tantamount to small, yet controlled, riots throughout two of four housing units. Inmates had blocked the main doors to the units with furniture and other items and were not confined to their cells, but moving throughout the common areas in an unfettered manner. Staff were able to make entry into these two units and bring inmates under control with little resistance. In one of the remaining two housing units, inmates offered no resistance and caused very little destruction.

The remaining unit, however, Unit 4, housed a particularly high concentration of knuckleheads who refused to submit in a peaceful manner. Consequently, a tactical decision was made to get staff on the roof, then cut holes in the sunlight, and drop munitions—flash bangs and sting balls—into the common area.

Flash bangs create an incredibly loud explosion designed to stun individuals and cause momentary confusion, thereby giving the tactical team time to gain the upper hand. Essentially, they are shockingly huge noisemakers and nothing more; they create no shrapnel nor contain projectiles of any sort and are used by SWAT teams and the military. Sting balls, on the other hand, do contain projectiles, which are in the form of small hard rubber balls that fire out in all directions. They look very much like a hand grenade and are activated in essentially the same manner.

Both flash bangs and sting balls are considered to be "less lethal" munitions, although they can cause serious injury.

The dynamic-entry plan entailed once the sting balls and flash bangs erupted throughout the unit, other staff would simultaneously breach the front and rear emergency doors of the unit and make a coordinated entry. Small groups of recalcitrant inmates—mostly the ringleaders of the disturbance—had set trash cans on fire, broken windows, destroyed furniture and recreation equipment, and fought tooth and nail as staff attempted to bring them under control, handcuff, and remove them from the units. By the time the fight was over, it was difficult to enter the unit without a self-contained breathing apparatus, as oleoresin capsicum ("pepper spray") hung thick in the air.

Once Unit 4 was brought under the complete control of staff, the facility was deemed secure and remained in lockdown status for days to follow. As the executive assistant to the warden at the time, once the facility was brought under control and deemed static, I quickly changed my clothes and addressed media representatives from Erie, Buffalo, and smaller outlets in relative close proximity of the facility. Quite understated, October 24, 1995, was one hell of a learning experience for my coworkers and me.

SUNNY CALIFORNIA

I had the good fortune of working in four different positions while at McKean, and by the time I left in 1997, I was promoted to associate warden at the Federal Correctional Institution, Lompoc, California, a low security level facility of about 1,500 inmates in one facility, and another 200 inmates or so in the adjacent minimum security level Intensive Confinement Center. The ICC was the Federal Bureau of Prisons' version of a boot camp and housed male inmates who had no history of violence and were considered low risk for recidivism. Interestingly, the bureau eventually shuttered all of its four ICCs due to the fact that long-term research revealed ICC "graduates" recidivated no less than inmates who had not gone through the program.

Lompoc was interesting and also a great learning experience for me. As one of two associate wardens, I had the opportunity to see what wardens went through on a daily basis. Plus, in the absence of the warden, the other AW and I alternated as acting warden, also an incredible learning experience. This forces new AWs to think big picture, communicate with the warden's supervisor—the regional director—and make relatively easy yet important decisions that affect the entire facility.

During my tenure as a new associate warden at Lompoc, our regional director arranged for all of the associate wardens in the Western Region of the bureau to visit and tour the famed San Quentin prison, which is part of the California Department of Corrections and Rehabilitation. Opened in 1852, San Quentin is the oldest prison in California and incarcerates inmates of all security levels. Although San Quentin's gas chamber hasn't been used since the mid-nineties when lethal injection was introduced as the method for executing those inmates condemned to death, it was extremely cool to see it. At the time of our visit, San Quentin housed around five thousand inmates which, from my perspective, is too many inmates in one facility, but that's how Cali does it. They have fewer prisons, but they're ginormous when compared with Bureau of Prisons facilities.

The Bureau typically assigns newly promoted associate wardens to lower level facilities as part of the acclimation process. After 18-36 months or so, if a first-time AW has proven his or her salt at that facility, most are laterally transferred to another federal facility of a higher security level. This stepping-stone process best prepares those who have been identified for eventual promotion into the warden ranks. Those who have not proven the ability to move up typically top out in the AW position for the remainder of their career.

Working at a low security level facility, FCI Lompoc was not a great challenge in terms of facing life-threatening situations, but really bad things can go very wrong even in low-level joints. There is more than one example throughout the Bureau's history when the wheels have come clean off at low security level facilities whereby full-scale riots erupted. However, when you have competent staff and, in particular, sound leadership, these things simply should not occur in those types of facilities.

It's important to describe in greater depth what the Special Housing Unit is and how it is utilized in a correctional environment. Different agencies have various official terms for the SHU ("shoo"), some call it the Restricted Housing Unit, the Security Housing Unit, etc., but in all cases the SHU serves as the isolation unit inside the prison. The SHU serves as the jail within the jail or prison, and inmates are typically locked up for twenty-three hours a day; the remaining hour for recreation in a small, isolated, self-contained area. The SHU is referred to staff and inmates by a host of slang terms: "the box," "the hole," and "the pokey" are but a few of the terms used to refer to the SHU. SHUs typically house inmates who fit into one of two categories: administrative detention and disciplinary segregation. The administrative detention component of a Special Housing Unit in the Federal Bureau of Prisons houses inmates who have not yet been found guilty of an administrative offense like fighting, possessing contraband, a positive drug test, or dozens of any other violations against prison rules. Inmates in administrative detention (AD) status include those who feel their safety is in danger due to anything from an unsatisfied drug or gambling debt, to being discovered as a pedophile, and anything in between. AD essentially houses inmates requiring separation—thus isolation—from the general population, pending the results of an investigation.

On the other hand, the disciplinary segregation (DS) component of the SHU houses inmates who have been found guilty of a rule violation and are serving the punitive aspect and/or awaiting transfer to a facility commensurate with their new security needs. Say at a low security level facility, an inmate severely injures another inmate with a weapon; clearly, the aggressor is no longer appropriate for a low security environment. He will therefore have his custody classification rescored and be transferred to, most likely, a medium security level facility. Because his actions demonstrated he is no longer appropriate for placement in a low security facility, he will be precluded from returning to the general population of the low security facility where he incurred the discipline. That same inmate will remain in the SHU until he is transferred to a medium secure facility and, at that time, will be permitted to be placed in general population.

During my tenure at Lompoc, we had a little person—a midget—of Mexican descent, who had a fiery temper. This dude got himself locked up in the Special Housing Unit due to being insolent with staff. Given the fact our little Mexican was an extreme hothead, he became more and more enraged due to being placed in the hole. As I was touring through the facility, as I did every day, I decided to go through the SHU.

As I entered the unit, the "seg lieutenant," who is the ranking staff member of the SHU, said to me, "Hey, boss, you should be hearing from the captain any minute because I just called him."

"Yea, what's up, lieu?" was my response.

The lieutenant said, "The little Mexican is *extremely* pissed, and he's throwing shit all over the cell." FCI Lompoc, being a low security facility, did not have a traditional special housing unit like one would see in a medium or high security facility. Rather, Lompoc's

SHU could house around only thirty-five inmates and did not have traditional single or two man cells, but larger bull pen–like cells that could accommodate five to eight inmates.

The little Mexican was in one of these larger cells with five or so other cellmates. I have to admit, it was one of the funniest things I had witnessed in corrections up to that point. Here was this midget, screaming and cursing—flailing about—I mean, really having a full-fledged temper tantrum. And all the while he's slinging his own turds all over the cell, and all these other much larger inmates did was lay low and do the best they could to avoid the literal shit storm!

* * *

Beautiful, sunny California is not without issues as I learned one gorgeous September Saturday afternoon while watching college football on TV at home. USP and FCI Lompoc sit on thousands of acres owned by the federal government; this property, and others similar to it throughout the agency, is typically referred to as a (federal) "reservation."

The reservation included the two main prisons, its respective satellite minimum security camp operations, a large training facility, and "reservation housing," which are dozens of houses and trailers that prison staff can rent at a somewhat discounted cost during their assignment at Lompoc.

The homes, many of which were mobile homes, for line staff and other nonranking staff were certainly not as nice as those of the facilities' ranking members, and the neighborhood was affectionately known as Tortilla Flats. Conversely, the modest yet beautiful houses with roomy yards and decks that were rented by department heads and institution executive staff of both prisons were situated up the hill from Tortilla Flats. This neighborhood was known as "Snob Hill."

As I was watching football, minding my own business, we heard a rather urgent knock at our front door. It was the penitentiary's chaplain who told us a wildfire was rapidly moving toward the reservation housing and the penitentiary warden—the highest ranking staff member at Lompoc—had ordered the evacuation of all staff living on Snob Hill.

My family quickly packed and went to a local hotel, along with the rest of the spouses and children of administrative staffs from the Federal Correctional Institution and United States Penitentiary.

Both prisons were located at least a mile from where the wildfire burned, but the reservation housing for staff, particularly on Snob Hill, was in real trouble as the fire was less than a quarter mile from the first row of homes.

We, along with minimum security level camp inmates, began digging shallow ditches which would, hopefully, serve as firebreaks. As the fire headed straight for the reservation housing, I saw a phenomena that freaked me out; had somebody told me it was possible, I wouldn't have believed it, but I witnessed the fire on one side of the road, and in an instant, it was suddenly burning on the opposite side of the road. The fire had literally jumped a two-lane road in the blink of an eye.

At any rate, we realized there was no way for us to save the homes that the fire was rapidly approaching and were about to abandon our efforts and accept our fate when, suddenly, the wind shifted and the fire headed in another direction. There was serious damage caused by that wildfire, but we were spared completely; in the end, there was no damage to staff housing, and no inmates or staff were injured.

* * *

As it turned out, being assigned to Lompoc as a first time associate warden proved to be one of the most educational periods of my career. Not only was I learning the ropes of my new position in the relative calm of a low security level facility, but Lompoc was a complex, meaning there was more than one facility on the vast acreage of the federal reservation. In addition to the FCI and its satellite Intensive Confinement Center, Lompoc was home to one of the biggest, bad-ass correctional institutions in the agency, and that was the United States Penitentiary, Lompoc.

USP Lompoc's perimeter fence was perhaps just a hundred yards or so from the FCI's perimeter fence, yet they were worlds apart in terms of the types of inmates that were housed there, and the level of violence that occurred with a high degree of regularity in the USP. It was home to some of the most violent offenders in the Bureau. My reporting date as a new associate warden at FCI Lompoc was April 6, 1997, three days after the most tragic day in USP Lompoc's history had occurred.

* * *

April 3, 1997, was a relatively peaceful day at the United States Penitentiary, Lompoc. Inmates and staff were going about their daily cycles when, at approximately 6:00 p.m. during an open, controlled movement through the facility's corridors, a piece-of-shit inmate, armed with a bone crusher and an ice pick–like shank, attacked Correctional Officer Scott Williams by sneaking up behind him and violently stabbing him in the neck with both weapons.

Officer Williams, just twenty-nine years old, a devoted husband and father and member of USP Lompoc's Special Operations Response Team, reached for his throat, staggered a few yards down the corridor, and collapsed, never to regain consciousness. He was pronounced dead at 6:55 p.m. As soon as the inmate stabbed Officer Williams, he immediately ran across the corridor and stabbed Officer Scott Elliot in the chest. Three other correctional officers who had immediately responded sustained minor injuries before the inmate was subdued and restrained.

USP Lompoc was never the same after that event, and it won't begin to be until every single staff member working there who was employed on that fateful day has retired. Just seeing what our brothers and sisters at the USP went through was gut-wrenching. Everything from the funeral—that United States Attorney General Janet Reno attended—to the lockdown period and return to "normal" operations was a horrible time. Seeing Officer Williams' wife and young children at the funeral and later at other institution events honoring Scott was simply too much for many staff to bear.

While heavy events were transpiring at the USP next door, I was dealing mostly with boring issues of little consequence, such as the report of an inmate demonic possession. While it sounds insane—and I will not argue that it isn't—the fact of the matter is that one sunny day in June, one of our Religious Services chaplains who, quite frankly, always struck me as a bit off, reported to the chain of command that an inmate had come to him and reported "having problems," to include nightmares. The chaplain sits down with the inmate in the facility's ecumenical chapel and begins to engage in a "counseling session" with him. Next, according to our whacky chaplain, as the inmate expressed the details of his charges relevant to being a "cho-mo," the chaplain "probed into the idea of him being molested as a child and his involvement with a witches' coven in Sacramento between the ages of ten and twelve years of age." As the inmate is describing being molested during these meetings, the chaplain stated that he "experienced feeling the presence of another spirit." Imagine a religious chaplain, no less an employee of a federal agency, reporting to his superiors that he was convinced evil spirits were suddenly at hand and involved in whatever experience he was having with this particular inmate!

According to the chaplain, subsequent to feeling this spiritual presence, he said, "If there was a spirit in this room other than the spirit of Jesus, would you identify yourself!?" The chaplain said that the inmate then "tensed up and spoke in a totally different voice, stating, "He is mine and you can't have him!" When the chaplain asked the spirit to identify himself, "he" identified himself as "Apollyon," and according to the chaplain, "described his conquests which I remembered described in the book of Revelation in the Bible." The chaplain goes on to say, "After a short exchange of words with Apollyon, it appeared that the inmate was lifted from the chair, turned in the air 180 degrees, and landed on the floor, facing in the opposite direction. He was totally tensed up and the voice of Apollyon was speaking. I commanded, 'By the blood of Jesus, I command you to let this man go!' The inmate immediately became limp." Of course, all of the staff involved in this situation after the chaplain had reported this "event" are looking around and at each other, as if to say, "Is this guy for *real*?!"

Unfortunately, it got crazier from there when the chaplain said the next thing that occurred was the inmate "tensed up again and the voice of Apollyon returned and two other voices manifested themselves, one of which who identified herself as a childhood friend of the inmate." The chaplain said that it was at that juncture that he "cast the demon out" of the possessed inmate. Call me a nonbeliever, but it was my distinct impression that the inmate was having some fun with the naïve chaplain.

United States Penitentiary, Lewisburg: Welcome to the Real World

After working at the Federal Correctional Institution, Lompoc, for about two and a half years, I was notified that I was being laterally transferred to the United States Penitentiary, Lewisburg, Pennsylvania. I was absolutely thrilled. Although a move from the position of associate warden at one facility into the same position at another facility was, technically, a lateral transfer, those familiar with internal bureau politics knew it meant something more.

From my perspective, the Federal Bureau of Prisons does a marvelous job of grooming, training, and preparing its staff for future positions of leadership through experience derived through incremental baby steps. There was never any way I could be considered, or properly equipped, to serve as warden of a high security level penitentiary someday without working at such a facility in a lower level position first. And up to this point in my career, which was about ten years, I had no experience in any of our high security penitentiaries. It was time to get my cherry busted.

USP Lewisburg, styled in Italian Renaissance architecture, opened its doors in 1932, and continues to serve as one of the bureau's major penitentiaries. As one approaches Lewisburg, he or she drives up a slight hill where beautiful pine trees symmetrically line each side of the road. Once you reach the front of the facility, you are rewarded with a view that is both beautiful and menacing. The facility's enormous smoke-stack protrudes high enough to be seen from just about any point in the quaint little town of Lewisburg, home to Bucknell University. Suffice it to say, the upper-crust, near–Ivy League college, and hard-core federal penitentiary serve as a glaring example of diametrically opposite entities, yet the local area prospers from both.

One can't help but think the facility is actually quite *beautiful*; yet the smokestack, combined with the thirty to forty foot perimeter wall including multiple gun towers, quickly reminds the viewer that this place is for real. Just a few of the facility's past infamous residents included Whitey Bulger, John Gotti, Henry Hill, Alger Hiss, Al Capone, and Jimmy Hoffa. USP Lewisburg is a facility that has seen a disproportionate amount of violence, mostly that of inmate on inmate, over the course of its history. Just outside the dining hall, which is located in front of the control center, and at a critical juncture where the facility's corridors meet, is a tile floor that I estimate to be a hundred or so feet in length and approximately fifty feet in width. The tile has a reddish hue and is simply known as "the red top" to inmates and staff. A great deal of blood has been spilled on the red top over the years, and only adds to the mystique of the United States Penitentiary, Lewisburg.

Much of the violence at Lewisburg stemmed from the so-called "race wars," which finds its roots in the 1960s and continued well into the 1990s, consisting primarily of white and black inmates. The race war in the Federal Bureau of Prisons really heated up when, in November of 1981, Thomas "Terrible Tom" Silverstein—the inmate who later would murder Officer Clutts at USP Marion—murdered a DC Black inmate named Robert Chappelle. Silverstein then murdered again, when in September of 1982, he murdered Raymond "Cadillac" Smith at USP Marion. Silverstein exacerbated his despicable act by dragging Smith's body along a range of cells in the Special Housing Unit, showing off what he had done. At this juncture, the bureau experienced a great deal of inmate-on-inmate violence—at least in its high security level penitentiaries—between white (primarily Ayran Brotherhood) and black (primarily Black Guerilla Family and/or the DC Black) inmates.

It's widely accepted that the white supremacist group, the Aryan Brotherhood, formed in California's prison system, specifically at San Quentin in the mid-sixties, in response to standing up to the Black Guerilla Family, which found its genesis in the infamous Black Panther, George Jackson. Prison gangs were, and are, formed not only for protection against violence, but also for power, respect, and entrepreneurial purposes; in other words, to move, control, and sell contraband (most typically drugs) and *make money*.

Members of the Aryan Brotherhood, or AB or The Brand, are typically easy to spot if you know what to look for in a correctional setting: handlebar mustaches and/or big, bushy beards, lots of tats—consisting of Nazi ideology, shamrocks, cloverleaves, or the numbers of 1–2, representing the first two letters in the alphabet, A and B—and, oftentimes, big muscles. They are Viking-like and look the part: big, bad, and not individuals you would typically want to mess with. The ABs, like many other prison gangs, are "blood in, blood out." In other words, the only way in to the gang is by murdering on the gang's behalf, and the only way out is to die. Prison gangs, much like the Italian and American Mafia, place *everything* of value below the gang…family, friends, job, status, all become secondary to absolute allegiance to the gang.

The ABs, as well as other serious gang members in any high security level prison demand respect; simply cutting a gang member off in the chow line, most often will lead to that individual being stabbed for such a blatant act of disrespect. And when an assault of this nature occurs, one that serves as punishment for an act of disrespect, it will usually be carried out in full view of staff and inmates, the most common location being the chow hall because it sends a clear message that the gang doesn't give a rat's ass who sees it; and that we are not to be fucked with. Serious gang members *hate* with a passion those who snitch, engage in homosexuality, and staff; although most of the time they don't beef with staff unless they feel thoroughly disrespected in some manner. They especially hate child molesters and those who perpetrate acts of violence or sex crimes on children.

In today's world of corrections, at least from my perspective, the ABs and other serious prison gangs are not motivated so much by racial hatred; it's more about power and control of the contraband coming into the facility, which equals money. Make no mistake, if one inmate from one gang disrespects one inmate from a rival gang, it's tantamount to disrespecting the entire gang, and all forces will be brought to bear against the entire other gang. As the saying goes, "Fuck with one, fuck with all."

In the midst of all the racial/gang violence in the mid-nineties, the DC Blacks murdered a white inmate at USP Lewisburg in December of 1996, thus exacerbating racial tensions within the high security level facility. In response, the ABs prepared for outright war and issued a TOS or "terminate on sight" order, which meant that all members had an open and continuous green light and obligation to kill any DC Black should the situation present itself. Interestingly enough, the ABs secretly communicated such orders from its three-member leadership commission to other members by utilizing invisible ink derived from their own urine. Once a letter was received, a source of heat—like a lighted match—was slowly waved under the letter from the sending member, and once sufficient heat was applied, the hidden message became barely visible and could be read by its receiver. And the message was all-out war against the DC Blacks. On August 28, 1997, "Big Al" Benton and other ABs viciously murdered DC Black inmates Frank Joyner and Abdul Salaam and stabbed another DC Black, Byron Ball, as the black inmates were playing a game of monopoly. The crime-scene photographs were grisly; it was a gruesome scene that nearly caused the decapitation of the murdered inmates. It caused the bureau to preemptively segregate members of the AB throughout other high security penitentiaries to ensure similar attacks did not occur there too. Undoubtedly, USP Lewisburg, as a high security level penitentiary, has historically incarcerated some of the bureau's very worst inmates.

Interestingly, however, at the present time, Lewisburg is designated as a Special Management Unit (SMU), which is an unusual category in terms of the types of facilities the Bureau of Prisons manages because it is reserved for inmates who, because of their inability to integrate in general populations at other high security penitentiaries, but are not "worthy" (at least not yet, anyway) of designation to the Admin Max (supermax), are designated to Lewisburg's Special Management Unit.

I worked at Lewisburg for a short period of time, only about a year and a half, but it was some kind of education. At the time of my arrival in 1999, it hadn't been but two years since the aforementioned event of August 28, 1997. During my tenure at Lewisburg, a few incidents stick out as being memorable for me. As one might expect, especially in a high security environment, the attempt by some inmates to obtain illicit drugs, either for personal use and/or sale, is continuous and invariably threatens the overall safety and security of the facility. I happened to be in the Health Services Department of the facility one afternoon when a radio call went out indicating a medical emergency, as it appeared an inmate was overdosing, presumably on a narcotic, and most likely heroin. The epidemic of opioid and heroin abuse that we know today was not a factor then because cocaine and crack cocaine were the prevalent drugs then, but heroin has always been a prison favorite. I suppose that's the case due to the mind-numbing effects that one derives from its abuse. Some inmates will do anything to "escape" the reality of a hardcore penitentiary.

When the inmate was brought into the medical area, he had no pulse; he was "flatlining," not breathing, and for all intents and purposes, was dead. The chief medical officer, who serves as the head physician in the facility, quickly administered Narcan to the inmate via injection. Narcan, which is the drug Naloxone, serves as an effective antidote for opiate overdose. Narcan works by blocking the potential deadly effects of opioids and is designed to actually reverse the overdose, which is typically marked by slowed breathing, etc. Within seconds of being hit with the shot of Narcan, the inmate opened his eyes, bolted into an upright seated position on the gurney he had been lying on, looked around at everybody in the room, and then without a word, lay back down and died immediately. He could not be brought back to life. The autopsy later confirmed what everybody pretty much already knew: heroin overdose.

* * *

Every week, Monday through Friday, during the noon meal throughout just about every Federal Bureau of Prisons' correctional facilities, upper-level administrators—including the warden—and all department heads engage in the same duty: standing mainline. Mainline is another unique tenet of the Federal Bureau of Prisons' culture. The term *mainline* comes from the designation of when the bulk of the prison's general population comes to the chow hall to stand in line for their meal, as opposed to "short lines," such as those who might be infirmed by being on crutches, in a wheelchair, etc. Short lines might be comprised of inmates on a specific work-detail, thus requiring them to receive their meals first and quickly return to work. The vast majority of the facility's population, however, is part of the "mainline;" consequently, nearly the entire inmate population will make their way through the chow hall.

The Bureau of Prisons discovered decades ago that it made good sense, primarily as a management tool, to have its administrators and department heads present and available at mainline to address inmate issues and concerns. This might sound rather liberal to a casual observer of correctional facilities, but, trust me, standing mainline is one of the most positive and effective ways to manage inmate populations. Simply by being present at an inmate mealtime and allowing inmates to approach and discuss issues with those in decision-making positions, creates an atmosphere of care, concern, responsiveness, and a genuine effort of doing the right thing by ensuring when an inmate has something coming, you ensure they get it. In the end, inmates realize that they are there *as* punishment, rather than *for* punishment.

This ultimately creates an overall safer and more secure environment. By no means should this practice be interpreted as weak or soft; when the answer is no, the answer is no, but staff should always take time to patiently explain why an inmate cannot have what he wants.

As I was standing mainline one day at Lewisburg, a radio call came over the air of shots being fired by one of the perimeter tower officers. It's a rarity, but one of our high security inmates was attempting to escape in broad daylight by scaling the perimeter's brick wall.

If you were to stand directly next to Lewisburg' perimeter wall, you'd swear there was no way an individual could find a way to scale it. There appear to be no suitable places to place one's hands or feet in order to be propelled toward the top. But it's amazing what human beings are capable of, especially in highly stressful situations. This guy attempting to escape was a short, lean and muscular type, really wiry and athletic, and supposedly had been a special-forces type at some point during a military career before his life headed in the wrong direction. You can imagine the shock of the correctional officer who was manning the tower closest to where this dude was trying to go over the wall. First of all, in reality, it is *extremely* rare for an inmate to attempt to go over the wall at any time, but especially during the middle of the day. And I have no idea what this guy was thinking because he had no plan in terms of what the hell to do *if* he made it over the wall alive. It just didn't make sense; it's quite conceivable he had had enough of Lewisburg and being locked up, and it was a flash of suicide by cop in an impulsive attempt to end everything. At any rate, this inmate, in true Spiderman-like acrobatic moves, somehow jumped up to reach a microwave head, which was ten to twelve feet from the ground. The head was part of the perimeter detection system, which was designed to break away once pressure of forty pounds or so is imposed; but it did not, and as the inmate was about to reach the top of the wall the closest tower officer opened fire with his M16 submachine gun. After popping off a handful of rounds, which all missed their mark, the inmate, apparently having reevaluated the reality of his situation, dropped to the ground—inside the wall—and assumed the position to be handcuffed. The inmate was taken to the hole and an investigation was immediately opened. As part of the bureau's protocol, the tower officer was relieved of his duties and replaced by another officer. The weapon he fired had to be examined, and the officer was escorted into the SIS's office to be interviewed about the event. I couldn't help but chuckle when the officer had been brought in, and he was obviously petrified with fear. Why? He was "out of uniform," in that he was wearing sneakers instead of bureau-approved black boots or shoes. That was the last thing on the warden's mind, but the officer actually thought he would be in big trouble, not over the appropriate attempt of exercising deadly force, but because he was wearing sneaks.

* * *

Although I was assigned to Lewisburg for a short stint, I witnessed many acts of violence there. One day I was standing mainline with fellow staff members. The facility was tense because we had just come up off a lockdown that morning. There had been a recent inmate assault of a member of one race against another, so that kind of thing, even when it's validated through intelligence gathering that bringing the facility "back up" will go smoothly, invariably causes prison staff to be a tad anxious. The morning meal had been served in a very deliberate and controlled manner, and there had been no issues, so we decided to serve the noon meal as we typically did… calling one block at a time.

As the large dining hall filled with inmates, everything appeared normal. Our Special Investigative Staff (SIS) were noting that everything looked as though coming off the lockdown would go well. The DC Black inmates sat in their area, the Aryans sat at the tables they normally sat at, and so on. The interactions between these various groups looked normal as well: there was no unusual quiet and/or posturing that one sees when tension in bubbling among various factions of inmates. As I stood in the back of the chow hall and chatted with a fellow associate warden, suddenly two Black inmates pounced on another Black inmate; this was something we hadn't expected, but it was on.

We saw no shanks or any other weapons but our reaction was immediate. I was about fifteen yards away from the melee and sprinted toward the three inmates. I body-slammed into them as hard as I could, with the four of us tumbling to the floor. My fellow associate warden jumped right in, and with the assistance of other staff, had the three inmates in cuffs within a few seconds. My warden later told me that he appreciated my willingness to jump in, but chided me for not taking time to adequately assess whether either inmate had weapons. He was right: lesson learned. I ended up with a broken finger and the other AW had a broken rib or two.

The same associate warden who had assisted in getting those three inmates under control was, a few years later, viciously attacked by an inmate in the very same chow hall at USP Lewisburg. This associate warden had been assigned to Lewisburg for quite a few years and had a stellar reputation among the inmate population for being fair, responsive, and professional. Nevertheless, some whack job of an inmate came up behind him one day, armed with a sissy-shank, and sliced his neck, attempting to cut his throat from one ear to the other. The AW was injured and has a lasting scar on his neck to prove it and was very fortunate to not have been killed, but to demonstrate that he would not be intimidated, as soon as he was stitched up, he was right back on the job and standing mainline. To me, this is a perfect example of the courage, dedication, and professionalism that the vast majority of correctional workers demonstrate almost routinely and without regard to personal concerns.

* * *

One afternoon at Lewisburg, a staff member in our prison factory dialed triple deuces because an inmate had stabbed another inmate in the neck with a screwdriver. As the inmate was being escorted by staff from the factory to the medical unit, the screwdriver he had been stabbed with was still protruding from his neck. The inmate was seriously injured but lived.

* * *

Probably the craziest thing that I witnessed or was involved in at Lewisburg had nothing to do with the inmate population, but was about the weather. We had experienced a few days of severe rain and subsequent flooding. I had never seen anything like it before. There is a portion of the roadway on the Lewisburg reservation that dips down a bit, creating a wide "U" shape in the roadway where the water was able to settle and accumulate. As the rain continued to pour, this area became increasingly worse, yet folks continued to drive through it.

Eventually, after so much continued rainfall, the area became impassible, but nobody knew just how bad it had become until a daughter of a staff member attempted to drive through it. Due to the high rushing water, the car stalled out and the young lady became stuck right in the lowest part of the dip in the roadway. Because it was raining so damn hard, water quickly entered the vehicle and began filling it. Rightfully panicked, the young lady scampered to the car's roof to seek refuge from the rising water. By this time, staff were being recalled to deal with the reservation flooding. Because I was living on the reservation at the time in a government house, I was literally a couple of hundred yards from where the young lady was stranded. When I arrived with some other staff, it was absolutely pouring the rain and the young lady was on the car's roof, a look of absolute terror written on her face.

With the increasing swiftness of the "creek," which by now was more like a river, nobody dared wading through the water to reach her at that juncture; it was simply too dangerous. Within a few minutes, however, one of our Facility Management staff had obtained a rope. Three of us "tied on," waded through the rushing water, and carried the young lady to safety. Later that day, one of our lieutenants became stranded in his pickup truck a few hundred yards from where the young lady had gotten jammed up. He also looked scared to death as he awaited rescue on the top of his truck. By that time, the raging waters were simply too much, and there was no way we were going to be able to reach him in the same manner as we had assisted the young lady. Eventually, a helicopter was called in and safely airlifted him from his truck.

* * *

The Federal Bureau of Prisons' high security penitentiaries in the beginning days of my career included Lewisburg, Lompoc, Marion, Terre Haute, Atlanta, and Leavenworth. It's an indisputable fact that violence perpetrated on staff can occur in a correctional facility of any security level. Similarly, it's a fact that the likelihood of an act of violence visited on staff by an inmate was most likely to occur in one of those great, big, hard-core penitentiaries. Lewisburg was one of those facilities in the bureau that had experienced the homicide of a staff member, which occurred on October 12, 1987. Sometime prior to that sad day in October 1987, during a visit at USP Lewisburg, an inmate and his wife orchestrated an escape plan. In accordance with the plan, the inmate intentionally inflicted what ostensibly was an accidental fall from his bunk bed, thus causing a head injury. In accordance with the conspiracy, the injury led to an escorted medical trip to the outside community hospital in Danville, Pennsylvania. Two confederates of the inmate lay in wait at the community hospital, one armed with a .25 caliber handgun, the other a .44 caliber pistol. The three escorting staff, including Officer Robert F. Miller, took the inmate inside the hospital where he was examined without incident. However, on the way back to the government vehicle, the staff were suddenly faced with the two armed gunmen who demanded that they halt; when they did not, the gunmen opened fire, striking what proved to be a fatal shot to the chest of Officer Miller. The inmate was liberated from the officers by his two accomplices, and they fled in a vehicle, which precipitated a high-speed chase by law enforcement. After eight miles or so, the grand escape plan came to a sudden halt when the escapee and his helpers crashed their vehicle and were taken into custody. Bobby Miller lost his life over that. He was married and had two young children. It makes me sick to think about it.

* * *

Its things like the death of Officer Miller or Officer Williams that cause you to wonder why things happen in the manner in which they do. You just think, "Why does shit like that happen?" Obviously nobody knows, and people attribute all kinds of reasons for why tragedies happen to good people, tragedies that have immeasurable ripple effects for years to follow. On the other hand, there are times when you think the stars have aligned just right based on some occurrence or another. One example of this type of thing occurred when I was the warden at the Metropolitan Detention Center, Brooklyn, New York. We had an inmate who was a serial "cho-mo" (child molester), undoubtedly the worst I have ever known in my career. One day, while on the toilet, he suffered a massive heart attack. Died right there on the crapper. It was one of those rare occasions when I thought to myself, *Good riddance*. At least he can't harm any more children.

* * *

With all of the violence that occurred inside the wall of USP Lewisburg, there were so many cool things about living in the town of Lewisburg in general, and on the USP's reservation in particular. Of particular note were the staff parties. As mentioned previously, BOP staff in general, but especially those that work in the dangerous environment of a high security penitentiary, tend to gravitate and hang with each other away from the job. Consequently, Lewisburg had all kinds of parties and fun family events. It wasn't unusual for the Employees' Club to take a trip to Pittsburgh for a Pirates game, or have a multitude of other family-oriented events on the federal reservation. The best example of a fantastic employees' event that I recall in my career is the annual Halloween Haunted House that the penitentiary's employees open to the community. All of the roles within the haunted house are filled by eager prison staff and a few spouses; quite frankly, it is the best, spookiest, haunted house you'll ever visit.

* * *

There are those times, like I experienced in my career when you don't wonder why something happened, primarily because in retrospect it's ultimately proven how an act or string of acts, typically involving monumental stupidity and/or greed, led up to a tragic event. The vast, vast majority of the Bureau of Prisons staff that I worked with throughout my career were decent, caring, ethical, and dedicated, correctional professionals.

To be certain, however, there is that tiny minority that goes the wrong way and, almost invariably, these individuals not only harm themselves, but their loved ones and fellow correctional workers too. Plus, they bring disrespect to the very admirable profession of being a correctional professional and perpetuate the stereotype that we're all just a bunch of dumb brutes with handcuffs and a propensity to use billy clubs.

From its inception in 1930, up until mid-2006, part of the Federal Bureau of Prisons' culture was to trust its staff until proven otherwise. Up until 2006, I had never come across or known of a jail and/or prison at the state or county level anywhere in America that *did not* search its staff when entering the facility at the beginning of shift change. The BOP was different. Up until then, BOP staff simply showed up for work, entered the facility carrying whatever he or she deemed necessary for their shift—lunch bags, coolers, whatever—and these items were never searched. Nor was the employee. He or she did not go through the process that we all go through today when processing through security at any airport. There was no emptying of the pockets, taking shoes and belts off, and/or randomly being patted down by a staff supervisor. That lack of trust simply wasn't part of the agency's culture, and frankly it was nice; but of course, there are those who took advantage of that trust, and it all came to a head on June 22, 2006.

The Federal Correctional Institution, Tallahassee, Florida, is located about three miles from downtown along Capital Circle Northeast. In 2006, Tallahassee's main facility was a low security level facility for females, with an adjacent administrative security level jail for men—the Federal Detention Center. Because Tallahassee's main inmate population was low security level females, it was considered one of the sleepiest facilities in the bureau. You almost never heard anything about Tallahassee, but on June 22 that all changed when a gunfight erupted in the lobby of the detention center, and ended just outside of the center.

As in other professions, lessons are learned the hard way sometimes, and this was certainly one of those watershed events in the bureau's history. Many things are done differently these days, but back then, it was not uncommon to have a male-dominated staff working in an all-female inmate facility. Not a good idea. Research clearly demonstrates that it's in the best interest of inmates, staff, and the overall safe operation of the correctional facility, to have mostly female staff working with female inmates, and mostly male staff working in a male inmate environment. This practice, in and of itself, is not without potential issues; nevertheless, undoubtedly, it decreases the chances of staff sexual misconduct.

On the morning of June 22, an agent of the Office of the Inspector General (OIG), along with agents of the Federal Bureau of Investigation (FBI), arrived at the facility with arrest warrants for six male correctional officers who had been indicted the day before for providing contraband to inmates in exchange for sexual favors, as well as intimidating inmates, which was designed to interfere with and cover up the investigation. Five of the six officers were taken into custody without incident; however, the sixth officer—given the lack of staff searches at that time—had secretly taken his personal handgun with him into the control center. The rouge correctional officer, Ralph Hill, rather than submit to arrest, fired upon the agents. The gun battle raged for a short time, but in the end, Hill was killed; the OIG special agent, William "Buddy" Sentner, was killed; and a Bureau of Prisons lieutenant was seriously injured when he was shot. It was one of the saddest days in BOP history because of the senseless loss of life, and it brought extreme negative attention to the agency, attention that, unfortunately, is so unfair when one considers the incredible good the vast majority of BOP staff engage in day in and day out.

Staff corruption, and the process that leads up to it, has always fascinated me. I don't think a brand-new staff member has ever walked into the facility where they've been newly hired and, by design, thinks how he or she could profit by engaging in criminal acts, acts that bring disrespect to the uniform and profession of corrections overall. No, the process of going "dirty" is typically a slow, methodical process that involves an inmate—or inmates—recruiting, cultivating, developing, and ultimately, exploiting the staff member.

Corrections, similar to other criminal justice professions, has a tendency to be a magnet for those who *love* power and enjoy being in positions where they exact control over others. In the end, these people will have a negative effect on the operation. In the extreme, their behavior can manifest in cases of excessive force and other forms of abuse. Aggressive personality types in corrections have a tendency to hate inmates and have strong feelings of judgment toward them, as they are unable to be professional, objective, and impartial in their dealings with them. Staff members that are passive also present a threat to the orderly operation of the facility, in that they are timid about enforcing rules and giving inmates direction and orders. These folks typically are not security-conscious and either not interested or able to observe the subtleties of inmate behavior that could warn of an impending disaster.

My experience is these folks are either intimidated or scared of inmates, and/or feel sorry for them and, eventually, become compromised. Predatorial inmates love these staff. They become a mark, a challenge for the inmate, and a potential means to sex, drugs, weapons, and communication with the outside world. It's no wonder that predatorial inmates use every trick in their collective bag to "turn" one of these staff members.

The third general personality is the assertive type. These were the folks I always attempted to hire. They know when to slide a bit toward the aggressive end of the spectrum and, conversely, when it's appropriate to move the other way on the scale by perhaps not enforcing minor infractions so vigorously. These folks employ common sense with alacrity, are constantly aware of their surroundings, and know when inmates are trying to play them. The professional and assertive staff member understands and does not judge different cultures, races, and religious practices; he or she is there to do a job well by understanding big-picture issues and what is important. These are the folks that are ideal for positions in the criminal justice system and certainly best suited for a career in corrections.

The *vast majority* of an officer's time is spent interacting with inmates; oftentimes a single correctional officer might be responsible for supervising upwards of a few hundred inmates. Therefore, it is *imperative* that all staff possess strong interpersonal skills, and have the ability to work, assertively direct, and control violent convicted felons from all walks of life. And I'll tell you, that ain't always easy.

In the early days of my career, there was a warden who told me how important it was to consistently hire staff who had good communication skills and the ability to invariably be completely fair with inmates. The warden put things in perspective for me by saying to imagine a riotous situation where the wheels are coming off and you lose control of the institution. He said, "Then imagine, will inmates come for you to take revenge? Or will most inmates step up and aid in your protection?" There have been many instances in institution riots where inmates protected staff from other hostile inmates because they respected them as fair and decent individuals. Conversely, there have been multiple instances where specific staff have been targeted and seriously abused by inmates in riotous situations. As you might imagine, the staff members that get themselves into trouble are typically at either far ends of the aforementioned personality spectrum. It's all about balance, good judgment, a sense of fairness, and enforcing the rules of the facility in their spirit, rather than their literal word. And because tangible weapons are typically not permitted within the secure perimeter of the facility, it is vital for staff to understand their best "weapon" is their ability to work with inmates in a professional and respectful manner, all while holding them accountable.

* * *

In terms of permitting members of the community to assist staff in its facilities, the Bureau of Prisons utilizes community volunteers in almost all of its facilities. Volunteers typically assist in religious services, education classes, drug treatment, and recreation activities. Administrators have mixed feeling about the use of volunteers; some good is definitely derived from the program but, conversely, others detest the program because it invites potential security issues. Most of the volunteers are there for spiritual-related purposes, and many naively believe they can bring out the good that they have come to believe is in every single inmate, regardless of what they have done or continue to do.

Every year at all BOP facilities where volunteers are utilized, the bureau celebrates their work by having a dinner and the warden passes out certificates to thank to all the volunteers. And, there is one special award bestowed on one worthy individual, the Volunteer of the Year.

During my tenure as associate warden at USP Lewisburg, on the very day that we were having our annual volunteer banquet, a communication between an inmate and one of our volunteers was intercepted and reported up through the chain of command. The volunteer, based on the communication, had expressed love and was to some degree or another romantically involved with the inmate. The volunteer in question was, yup, our Volunteer of the Year that would have been announced at the banquet that evening. Suffice it to say, we presented the award to another volunteer while terminating future visits by the corrupt volunteer.

CITY OF BROTHERLY LOVE

In 2000, I was promoted to the position of deputy regional director, in the bureau's Northeast Regional Office in Philadelphia, Pennsylvania. In my new position, I was responsible for the supervision of fifteen or so administrators who provided technical support to the field of the nineteen facilities in the region and acted as a liaison between the regional director and the nineteen wardens in the region. It was a great learning experience because on a daily basis I saw what was expected of wardens from their boss—the regional director—who was my boss as well. Plus, I saw the various and wide-ranging issues that confronted all of these wardens who were in our region.

I had barely been in the position of deputy regional director for a few short months when, in November 2000, a vicious attack of a correctional officer took place at one of the facilities in our region, the Metropolitan Correctional Center, New York. MCC New York is a high-rise pretrial/presentence facility, so like MDC Brooklyn, its mission is that of a jail and classified as an administrative facility, meaning it holds inmates of all security levels. The key difference between Brooklyn and the MCC is that the MCC is considerably smaller (around 750 inmates).

The MCC, activated in 1975, has a history of incarcerating many infamous inmates, including drug kingpin Frank Lucas, John Gotti, Bernie Madoff (prior to sentencing), and terrorists such as Ramsi Yousef and Omar Rahman. In fact, subsequent to being extradited to the United States, escape artist and Mexican drug kingpin "El Chapo" Guzman was incarcerated there pending the outcome of the case against him.

One of the most interesting aspects of the MCC is the fact that when inmates are transferred from the jail to the courthouse in lower Manhattan, which is across the street, once placed in full restraints, inmates proceed through a tunnel that connects the two buildings. This is a security measure that has proven to be quite effective in terms of enhancing the safety and security of inmates and Bureau of Prisons and United States Marshall Service staff. Before most Americans had ever heard of Osama Bin Laden, in November 2000, a top al Qaeda lieutenant, Mamdouh Mahmud Salim, was being detained at the MCC on charges in connection with terrorist conspiracy attacks of at least two United States embassies in Africa where hundreds of people were killed.

On November 1, while being housed in unit 10-South, Salim had concealed a small plastic comb that he had repeatedly sharpened in his cell by rubbing it on a hardened surface. Salim's plan was to kill as many staff as possible, gain access to cell keys, then free as many inmates as he could while taking staff hostages. It was an unrealistic and stupid plan, but he was in fact able to wreak havoc by seriously assaulting Correctional Office Louis Pepe. When Salim's cell door was opened, Salim and his cellmate sprayed hot sauce in Pepe's face then proceeded to stab him in the eye and head. Pepe was then severely beaten before the two inmates were subdued by other staff, but not before seriously injuring Officer Pepe, who lost an eye and suffered permanent brain damage. For this assault, Salim received a prison sentence of thirty-two years and is incarcerated at the Bureau of Prisons Supermax facility in Florence, Colorado.

As previously mentioned, the worst thing that can occur in a correctional facility is the homicide of a staff member, but the *greatest failure* in corrections is the escape of an inmate from secure custody. This doesn't include a "walk away" from a minimum security environment, although that too is technically an escape; no, I'm talking about when an inmate has successfully defeated the physical barriers, such as fences, concertina razor wire, gun towers, armed perimeter officers, etc., in order to effectuate such escapes.

I was fortunate to have never worked in a facility that experienced an escape during my time there. And while escapes from secure custody are extremely rare, they do occur, and when they do, it is totally defeating to the staff that work at that facility. During my tenure in the BOP's Northeast Regional Office, the Bureau of Prisons—in my region—experienced an escape from the Federal Correctional Institution, Elkton, Ohio. On July 21, 2001, two inmates escaped by scaling the perimeter fence with a ladder that had been fashioned from a hospital gurney. It was a significant event and sent shock waves throughout the agency in that it *was* an escape from secure custody at a BOP facility. However, there was a mitigating factor in the event, and that was the fact the bureau had recently fenced the satellite, minimum security level prison camp, which sat next to the main, low security level Federal Correctional Institution. But because of the decision to fence the satellite facility, it technically elevated its security level from a minimum camp to a low security level facility, although at that time it contained mostly minimum security level camp inmates, interspersed with some low security level inmates.

* * *

Two other incidents occurred during my time at the bureau's Northeast Regional Office that have stayed in mind. The first was a brief hostage-taking of a correctional officer by a high security level inmate at the United States Penitentiary, Allenwood, Pennsylvania. I received a call from the warden from USP Allenwood one morning, who was screaming something about a staff hostage situation. Once I could discern what he was saying, it was obvious that an inmate had taken a staff member at knife point in one of the penitentiary's housing units, inside the correctional officers' office. The hostage situation ended almost as quickly as it had begun. In short order, one of the associate wardens at the facility orchestrated a dynamic entry on the office where the officer was being held, and the inmate was quickly subdued without injury to the officer, hostage taker, or anybody else.

The other incident was 9/11. On that fateful Tuesday morning, my supervisor, along with the rest of the agency's executive staff, including the director, assistant directors, and the other five regional directors, were in their quarterly executive staff meeting in Washington, D.C. A staff member had run into my office and said a plane had hit one of the World Trade Center towers in Manhattan. We flipped on the television in my office and began to watch the situation unfold. We witnessed on live TV—like so many other Americans—when the second plane hit the other tower. It was obvious in that moment this was an act of terror. We quickly assembled a staff meeting and strategized how we could best provide support to all the facilities in our region, especially the Metropolitan Correctional Center, New York, located in lower Manhattan, and the Metropolitan Detention Center, Brooklyn, New York.

Although it never came to fruition, we needed to develop emergency plans for potentially moving inmates from both of these facilities, whose total population was about three thousand inmates. In the panic that ensued after the Pentagon was hit by a third airliner, many of our line-level administrative staff in the office were practically sprinting out of the building where the Northeast Regional Office is located, the United States Custom House, in "Old City" Philadelphia, fearing that a governmental building in a major city could potentially be targeted. As events of that day unfolded, it felt as though the entire nation was under attack and destruction was imminent. Most staff simply wanted to get the hell out of the building and go pick up their children.

On October 17, 2001, I was sent to MCC New York, the high-rise federal jail in lower Manhattan, on an unrelated matter. During my visit, a few of the MCC staff took me on a "law enforcement only" car-ride through the destruction of the World Trade Center towers. No civilian vehicles were permitted to drive on the law enforcement-designated path that went through and around the thousands of tons of massive, twisted steel beams that had once erected and supported the twin towers. I'll never forget the sights and sounds of that day. Although it had been about five weeks since the attacks, the debris still smoldered and smoked, releasing a sickening burning smell that's difficult to articulate.

When our vehicle arrived at the end of the path, a team of hazard material individuals in full "hazmat" gear stood ready to hose our car down to assure no coating of the burning residue remained on the vehicle. Although it was mid-October and had been some six weeks since the disastrous event of 9/11, the memory of the ride through the debris field and the look and demeanor of the folks working at the site is something that will always stay with me.

* * *

During my time in the Northeast Regional Office of the Federal Bureau of Prisons, the infamous incident of "Spermgate" came to light. Four of the many correctional facilities within the Northeast Region at that time included those of the Federal Correctional Complex, Allenwood, Pennsylvania. Allenwood is designated as a "complex" because multiple facilities are situated on the same federal reservation. The Federal Prison Camp, Allenwood, a minimum security level facility, was the first federal facility to come under the name of Allenwood. It was the sole Allenwood facility for years until the low security level Federal Correctional Institution, the medium security level Federal Correctional Institution, and the high security level United States Penitentiary were constructed and activated in the early 1990's.

In 2002, Spermgate was revealed to the public, which was an embarrassment to the entire Federal Bureau of Prisons. For a period of approximately two years, a New York organized crime member and his wife were paying a correctional officer at the low security level facility to smuggle the inmate's semen from the prison and then delivered to his wife outside the facility, so that she could become pregnant. Some state systems allow conjugal visits, which, if an inmate demonstrates positive adjustment and behavior, he/she is permitted to shack up for a designated period of a few hours to engage in sexual activity with his/her spouse.

The use of conjugal visits always went against my grain, especially when I was much younger. I figured if you did the crime, missing out on one of life's greatest pleasures was simply too bad. However, as I've gotten older and wiser, I've come to view conjugal visits as potentially being one hell of a management tool that could be utilized to modify inmates' behavior, but the feds' view has always been that a lack of sex with one's spouse is one of the punitive measures inflicted on the convicted, thus serving as a deterrent to come to prison. The fact of the matter is there are a number of state correctional agencies that have had extremely good results in utilizing conjugal visits as a means of modifying inmate behavior. Moreover, I would argue that those who engage in criminal activity don't think that far ahead, nor do they think they will be caught, let alone prosecuted, found guilty, and actually serve hard time. With all of the violence that occurs in correctional facilities, particularly in high security prisons, it strikes me that a management tool of this nature could potentially lead to a decrease in overall violence and sexual assaults. At any rate, the feds have never permitted conjugal visiting.

The corrupt correctional officer was receiving about $300 per trip of semen out the front door when, lo and behold, another woman who claimed to be the girlfriend of another inmate said that she would pay him as much as $5,000 to bring her boyfriend's semen out of the facility for her to use to become pregnant. It turns out the higher paying girlfriend was an undercover officer and her inmate "boyfriend" was cooperating in an investigation designed to root out staff corruption at the facility. The dirty correctional officer eventually donned a prison uniform himself, as he was sentenced to twenty-seven months in prison. Three other correctional officers were charged and indicted as well, all of whom eventually pled guilty to smuggling into the facility mostly "soft" contraband items such as food, toiletries, and watches.

THE WARDEN'S DESK

In the spring of 2002, I received the message I had been waiting for my entire career: I was being promoted to the position of warden. In terms of pay, moving from the deputy regional director position to a warden's desk was, technically, a lateral move in that my grade and pay would not change, but it was a huge step. Wardens in the Federal Bureau of Prisons earn the official United States Office of Personnel title of "chief executive officer," and from my perspective the title fits. Wardens are, ultimately, solely responsible for the overall safety and security of their facility. The warden is charged with ensuring the care, control, and custody of all inmates, as well as the recruitment, retention, training, development, and hiring and firing of all of his/her staff. Moreover, the warden is responsible for the mood, tone, and tenor of the facility, fiscal management, community relations, building and strengthening relations with members of the judiciary, law enforcement and other correctional entities that exist nearby. It's a big job. Plus, to receive a promotion at the executive level (GS-13 and above), the Bureau of Prisons' entire executive staff must approve the promotion, as it only takes one individual to negate the entire deal.

Approximately four times each year, the bureau's executive staff gets together at various locations but, more often than not, at the Central Office—headquarters—in Washington, D.C. There, the "exec staff" meets for three or four days and reviews a multitude of issues involving all critical agency decisions such as staffing levels, budgets, construction, and the policy implementation of new laws enacted by Congress, etc. At the conclusion of the aforementioned items for discussion, the exec staff invariably conducts "personnel moves," which is a type of horse-trading of institution executive level staff all over the agency. Those typically in attendance at bureau exec meetings, include seven assistant directors, six regional directors, and the director.

Assistant directors serve as agency division heads and are assigned to the Central Office, as they serve largely as policy makers and advisors, but technically have as much clout as their counterparts, the regional directors, and there are six of them, each representing one of the agency's regions. While assistant directors and regional directors are considered equals, and are part of the same pay scale—the Senior Executive Service (SES)—the fact of the matter is that regional directors are more powerful because they are the ones that supervise the wardens who supervise the facilities, and therefore have much greater control over who gets promoted and where those folks will be assigned. The interesting thing, however, is that when a name is put before the agency's "exec staff" by any of its members, *all* other members must agree before the director officially approves the move. Staff selections at that level must be unanimous.

Invariably, during the week of each exec staff meeting, all of the facility staff at the executive level in the field are on pins and needles and, quite literally, hundreds of phone calls take place because staff are talking to their buddies in the field, doing their very best to get the latest scoop on rumors about who might be going where, who might be on their way to some primo job versus who has recently screwed up and might be on their way down the ladder. It's an interesting dynamic that's a big part of the bureau's culture.

From my perspective as a two-time associate warden and deputy regional director, I had a clear vision of how I wanted to accomplish my goal of being a successful warden. As part of the Bureau of Prisons' culture, the warden holds a "morning meeting," without fail, Monday through Friday. The morning meeting is comprised of the facility's leadership team within the institution, known as the institution executive staff. The institution executive staff typically includes the warden, one, two, or three associate wardens, depending on the size, mission, and complexity of the facility; the executive assistant to the warden and/or the camp administrator, who is in charge of the satellite, minimum security level camp; and the captain, the highest ranking member of the biggest department in the facility, the Correctional Services Department.

During the morning meeting, the warden first calls on the captain to provide a brief rundown of all important issues and events that have occurred over the last twenty-four hours (or weekend). The captain will describe all acts of violence while providing insight derived through investigation and intelligence, attributing causation and possible future ramifications. If we had a simple fistfight between two white dudes, and during the course of the investigation both inmates said it was over whose turn it was to empty the garbage from their cell, well, that's one thing. Conversely, it's a much different thing when we learn that three inmates requested protective custody the night before because they all said a shit storm between the Mexicans and African American inmates was about to kick off due to drug or gambling debts. How the warden directs and manages these everyday situations can have very serious consequences; underreacting is potentially just as dangerous as overreacting to any given situation. After the captain's briefing, the warden calls on all other meeting participants to provide the same kind of synopsis of issues and events occurring in their respective areas of responsibility. Suffice it to say, the morning meeting is key to the overall successful operation of the facility because it promotes communication and teamwork, identifies and highlights current events and issues, and allows the warden to assess the strengths and weaknesses of his or her executive staff.

In every situation when I came in as a new warden of a facility—five in all—I made it a point within the first month of my arrival to meet individually with every supervisor and department head. This included anywhere between twenty and forty individuals and was quite time consuming, but it assisted immensely in helping me figure out who was who and what they were all about. It helped me in determining if the wheels ever came off, who I would want in my corner, and who I would want making crucial decisions in the event I became incapacitated.

* * *

Another cultural tenet of leadership in the Federal Bureau of Prisons is what is fondly referred to as MBWA. MBWA is an abbreviation that we heard at wardens' conferences every year, as well as throughout an entire career. MBWA, or management by walking around, is perhaps the single most important function of the warden or, for that matter, any other individual in a position of leadership in the facility. The only thing you have to rely on is what other staff are telling you about something tangible if you don't get your ass out of the ivory tower and go put an eyeball on it for yourself. As the warden, it's imperative that you know the physical layout of the facility, what door leads to the outside of the unit, where a range or corridor will take you; will it lead to a dead end? Or is there a safe haven somewhere in the area if things get ugly? That's one of the many reasons why wardens need to know their physical plant, but there are many others too. Visibility is extremely important for the warden of any correctional facility, and there are a multitude of reasons for that. When staff and inmates see the warden strolling through the facility, it tells them a great deal. For the staff, it indicates the warden is not some pencil pusher that sits at his/her desk all day. Staff want to see their leader, as the famous sportscaster Keith Jackson might say, "Down in the mud and the blood with the big uglies." It demonstrates a willingness to get "out there" in the areas where things have the potential to go bad—the recreation yard, the chow hall, the Special Housing Unit, etc. And from a personal perspective, I always thought it was important to tour the facility by myself. I always had underlings that wanted to tag along, but wardens gain more credibility when they don't have an entourage hanging with them. Although it may not be true, the act of having subordinate staff walk with the warden throughout the facility is perceived as weakness by inmates and arrogance by staff. Inmates think you're afraid, and staff think you're too good to walk alone.

Plus, inmates and staff are much more prone to approach the warden when he or she is out walking alone. I learned all kinds of interesting things about inmates, staff, and the overall operation of the facility simply by being on the compound by myself every day. There were many times during my tenure as warden when I would say something about an individual or situation at one of our meetings, and my executive staff would look at me and say, "How the hell did you know that?" My response was the same every time, "All staff members should have a good snitch or two."

Walking the facility also provides wardens and other administrative officials the opportunity to teach and train staff, make procedural corrections on the spot, as well as develop potential confidential inmate sources. One of the things that my executive staff and I constantly attempted to drill into the heads of our staff, was the vast importance of performing the basics well. When staff avoid complacency and apathy and, conversely, focus on the basics of the job, the likelihood of negative events happening is diminished. Basics include, but are not limited to, key control, performing inmate counts the correct way, tapping bars to ensure they haven't been weakened by an inmate attempting to diminish their structural integrity, inmate accountability on job sites and housing units, tool control, conducing thorough shakedowns (searches) of inmates and areas, recognizing and reporting unusual behavior, and so many others. In every executive staff meeting, department head meeting, union meeting, and any other meeting, I felt that it was part of my job to speak about the basics and their importance.

* * *

In 2002, I found myself back in sunny Santa Barbara County, where the climate is damn near perfect, at the facility where I first made associate warden, the Federal Correctional Institution, Lompoc, California. It was by pure coincidence that I returned to a facility that I had worked at previously, and I was very happy to be back, not only because my family loved the central coast of California, but also because FCI Lompoc, being a low security level facility, from my perspective, was still the well-oiled machine that I had come to know in 1997 through 1999. It was great to be back for personal and professional reasons. FCI Lompoc was an ideal facility for a new warden to get his/her feet wet, and the facility certainly provided me with that experience, but the real learning experience lay just next door at the high security level United States Penitentiary, where Officer Scott Williams had been murdered five years earlier.

* * *

I was enjoying a weekend day off when I saw staff POVs (personally owned vehicles) tearing down the hill on the federal reservation where many institution executive staff from both facilities resided. It was obvious that the penitentiary had an emergency of some sort and a multitude staff were responding to the facility. I wasn't asked, but I drove the half-mile or so from my house to the main entrance to the penitentiary and asked the officer at the front desk if I could help in any way. Once cleared to enter the facility, I walked with a senior correctional officer out to the recreation yard where a melee had just been brought under control that occurred between Caucasian and African American inmates.

There were about thirty dudes, both white and black, who were lying face down or seated on their butts, handcuffed, and bloody. There were a handful of shanks that were plainly visible on the ground too. In high security level correctional facilities, especially on a recreation yard where there are potentially upwards of a thousand inmates and the likelihood of violence most prevalent, when things go bad and various factions of inmates decide to go to war, you'll see inmates squat down and coughing in order to retrieve shanks—homemade knives—from their rectal cavity. The white boys—at least in this tussle—got their asses kicked. While there were no deaths or life-threatening injuries, there was a lot of blood and ugly facial wounds. Given that the issue involved a multitude of inmates, exacerbated by the interracial fact, meant a total lockdown of the facility.

The locking down of a correctional facility is a major pain in the ass. It's stressful to staff and inmates, is costly, and entails a painfully slow and methodical process that has to occur before determining whether or not the facility can safely be brought back to normal operations. When something occurs in a correctional facility that precipitates a lockdown, the process usually unfolds in similar manner. When present, only the warden can authorize a lockdown in the Bureau of Prisons. The exception is in the absence of the warden, his or her actor can make that call, and when the institution's executive staff is not in the facility—such as weekends, evening and morning shifts, and holidays—the individual who can make that call is the operations senior lieutenant, who serves as the shift supervisor. However, that same lieutenant had better get the warden on the phone as soon as absolutely possible.

Subsequent to the decision to lockdown, the control center officer will make an announcement over the public address system by stating, "Recall! Recall! All inmates return to your housing units!" This means to all inmates they are to immediately drop whatever it is they're doing at the time and return to their housing unit and, more specifically, their cell.

Once all inmates are recalled and locked into their cells, invariably, an emergency count ensues. This unscheduled count is conducted to eliminate the worst possible scenario first: a missing or escaped inmate. Once the control center officers, in conjunction with the lieutenant, determine there is a "good count," then the rest of the process is much less urgent and stressful and can proceed methodically.

When bad shit goes down in correctional facilities, the most important factors include isolating and containing the situation, and accounting for all inmates and staff. Once those things are accomplished, there is a host of other checklist items, depending on the severity of the situation, that must be followed. If the wheels have really come off, the warden must consider actions such as recalling off-duty staff, removing all visitors, volunteers, and contractor staff from the facility and notifying outside law enforcement and his/her chain of command regarding the situation. The Command Center will be activated and manned by prison staff trained and designated in advance of such an event. There, they will review video tape, if applicable, of the significant event, listen to inmate recorded phone calls, and discuss and develop strategies for handling the specific nature of the event. In a lockdown situation, mass interviews take place, meaning that *every* inmate in the facility is briefly interviewed. In doing so, no inmate or group of inmates is singled out, and therefore subject to being labeled as a snitch. Plus, you never know what intelligence might be gleaned by interviewing every inmate.

Depending on the nature of the incident, the warden may want to consider more extreme measures such as disabling televisions and inmate telephones, placing extra staff on the perimeter, disabling utilities, equipping trained staff with video cameras, and activating the facility's command center. Sack meals will continue to have to be prepared three times a day by staff for the entire inmate population who, rather than eat in a chow hall, will receive their meals in their cells. If an act of violence has been perpetrated, crime scene preservation is crucial, as well as the activation of emergency response teams like the Special Operations Response Team and Disturbance Control Teams. If necessary, tactical assault plans must be drawn up, including less lethal and lethal options, then rehearsed and practiced in the event a dynamic crisis response becomes necessary.

An established triage area may need to be prepared in the event there are multiple injuries. Conducting mass interviews, addressing the media, communicating with agency executive staff, removing inmate instigators from the population, and conducting staff briefings are but a few of the many things the warden must carefully evaluate and execute.

Once the crisis is over, resuming normal operations is not quite as simple as one might think. Bringing a facility "back on line," or back to normal operations, is a process of incremental steps. Effective communication with inmates must occur, and typically I found that a simple memorandum explaining why we were locked down and what the plan was for coming back online was the most effective method to get our message out. Communication from staff to inmates is always imperative in lockdown situations.

When situations of violence occur, particularly those that cross races, coming off the lockdown can be particularly tricky. The facility's administration must depend on the intelligence derived from mass interviews, telephone conversations, and what our "snitches" are telling us, and from that information construct a plan for how the facility will resume normal operations.

Oftentimes, in tense situations like that, it's best to bring the facility back online in a very slow and controlled manner. For example, you might start by letting inmates out on the ranges or tiers of a housing unit before allowing the entire unit to be released. Or the warden may approve a plan that designates units, or half units, to proceed to the chow hall, rather than releasing inmates in larger groups. In bringing a facility back online in this incremental fashion, it allows staff to observe inmate behavior while simultaneously allowing inmates to "sniff" each other. The term is used in the context of how dogs, wary of each other, sniff the others before deciding if they're going to attack. Oftentimes, the "sniffing" process allows inmates—particularly the leaders—to intermingle and talk and, hopefully, resolve any lingering issues that could lead to more violence.

Because lockdowns are tricky, you had better know what the hell you're doing when you execute a lockdown and, again, when you bring the facility back to normal. It's sort of like mountain climbing, in that it's well and good when the climber makes it to the summit of Mount Everest, but the danger has just begun at that point, and the tricky part of the deal is returning back down the mountain. Lockdowns are tense and dangerous situations and, quite literally, can be the difference between life and death.

The lockdown of a correctional facility is something that should be taken extremely seriously by corrections administrators and should occur with reason and logic that inmates and staff can understand. When a facility is locked down—and there could be dozens of reasons for ordering one—it is imperative that it be executed as expeditiously as possible. The longer it takes for a joint to go down, staff control is diminished, and the chance for a lack of cooperation on the part of the inmate population is increased. Furthermore, as long as the security of the facility is not further jeopardized, revealing the purpose of the lockdown should be made known to staff and the inmate population as soon as practical. In general, it will be fairly obvious why a facility is "going down," especially when there is, for example, a loud fight involving multiple inmates, etc., but communication will be essential as any crisis unfolds in a correctional facility. It is incumbent upon the warden to know how and when to deliver pertinent information to staff and inmates. This, from my perspective, is best accomplished by conducting staff briefings as frequently as possible, and with inmates, I have found it most effective to communicate in the form of the aforementioned memoranda to the entire inmate population. Subsequent to any lockdown, I would instruct my team to discuss, develop, and write this memo as a group. Once I had approved and signed the final version, it would be copied and hand-delivered by staff to each inmate in every cell throughout the entire facility. Communication from the leadership of the facility to inmates and all staff is absolutely essential to the successful lockdown *and* return to normal operations.

On the other hand, however, the facility could be locked down because an escape plot was uncovered, and even though you can't reveal the reason for the lock down, you have to do your best to communicate to the population that every effort will be made to bring the facility back to normal as soon as practical. As is usually the case in most human situations, communication is the key. The reputation and trust the warden has established with the inmate population is paramount.

In most, but certainly not all cases, lockdowns are a result of violence perpetrated by an inmate (or inmates) against another inmate (or inmates). At times, however, inmates are violent toward staff, and any time a serious attempt, or actual act of violence is perpetrated against a staff member, the facility will be locked down. I experienced many lockdowns over the years, and there are definitely a few that stick out as being memorable and, in some cases, rather dramatic.

* * *

In 2004, sometime during my first assignment as a warden at the Federal Correctional Institution, Lompoc, California, a disturbance erupted in K Dorm of the penitentiary next to my low security facility in the high security United States Penitentiary. As previously mentioned, in those days USP Lompoc was considered one of the two or three most dangerous and violent facilities within the Federal

Bureau of Prisons. There were constant issues relevant to race, gangs, and the control and distribution of hard contraband (mostly drugs) in the facility.

On this particular late afternoon, inmates—mostly Mexicans—began to become unruly, primarily because many of these inmates were intoxicated from ingesting homemade alcohol ("hooch").

Correctional facilities, particularly those of higher security level, are dangerous places as is; add alcohol to the mix and you've got quite a shit storm brewing on your hands. I have found that, almost invariably, when correctional administrators begin locating hidden alcohol (but not necessarily other types of drugs) during shakedown searches, etc., there is little doubt that violence is sure to follow. Alcohol, testosterone, and criminality make for a dangerous combination.

On this particular occasion, inmates were becoming agitated, argumentative, and in some cases, were showing obvious signs of intoxication; therefore, the operation lieutenant—who serves as the shift commander—made the decision to order all K Dorm inmates into their cells from the common areas. When the inmates refused to rack into their cells, the operations lieutenant made the call—in the absence of the warden—to lockdown the facility. As the lieutenant was directing officers, ordering inmates into their cells, and notifying the control center that the entire facility was to be placed on lockdown, the situation was quickly spinning out of control. As inmates became more and more emboldened due to liquid courage, they also became more hostile and violent. Approximately fifteen inmates then surrounded the unit manager of K Dorm and simultaneously assaulted the lieutenant and a chaplain—a Muslim Imam (spiritual leader)—who happened to be in the unit at the time. The chaplain had been sucker-punched by an inmate and was knocked completely unconscious. Making matters much worse by compromising security, some of the intoxicated inmates were able to wrestle the unit keys away from a correctional officer in the melee.

At that point, the entire facility was being locked down in a controlled manner while K Dorm's wheels had come damn near clean off. The lieutenant and chaplain were trapped in the unit and one correctional officer was unaccounted for. Exacerbating the issue, the riotous inmates had barricaded the front door to the unit off one of the main corridors in the penitentiary. One of the penitentiary's associate wardens was able to get inside the prison and to K Dorm to observe the situation. After making a quick assessment, the associate warden called for the "crash cart." The crash cart in the world of corrections is, quite literally, a cart with wheels that can be hustled throughout the facility when needed; in essence, it is a rolling armory, as it contains pepper spray, sting balls, flash bangs, riot batons, and less lethal guns capable of launching beanbags, gas, and other projectiles designed to bring violent situations under control.

As the remainder of the facility was being locked down, staff were better able to devote the majority of their attention to resolving the issue in K Dorm. Once the facility was locked down, officers began suiting up in riot gear and responding to K Dorm. Once the associate warden—who was the acting warden at this point—determined that he had enough staff to enter the unit, he quickly developed a tactical assault plan and it was executed. Within minutes, the chaplain, lieutenant, and missing officer were located and extracted from the unit and the unit keys were located. I remember seeing the lieutenant shortly after he got out of the unit and his entire face and head, and much of his Bureau of Prisons uniform shirt, were covered in blood. In all, seventy-eight rounds of OC gas, sting balls, and beanbag rounds had been utilized in quelling the violence and bringing the unit back under control.

* * *

Also during my tenure as warden of the Federal Correctional Institution, Lompoc, California, one of the most dramatic episodes of inmate violence erupted once again at the penitentiary next door. One Friday evening in the United States Penitentiary's gymnasium, the vast majority of Black inmates present initiated various posturing by physically squaring off and talking shit to each other. The violence kicked off rather suddenly and severely, as the homemade weapons seemingly appeared out of nowhere. If you've never seen a bunch of pissed-off felons who are doing significant time, suddenly bearing weapons resembling those used during the Crusades, it does tend to get your attention. As fate would have it, when this particular shit storm unfolded, the only staff member that was actually present was one of the penitentiary's three associate wardens. On any other Friday evening, between recreation and correctional services officers, there would be at least two or three staff present, but this was not any other Friday evening.

The driving force behind this melee was originally believed by staff to be between the violent street gangs of Los Angeles, the Bloods and the Crips. That logic makes perfect sense, but that was not what precipitated this event. No, it actually happened to be an internal business issue within another SoCal (Southern California) street gang, the Dirty South. When the violence went down, some Crips went one way while some Bloods went the other way. Then, things got especially ugly when the shanks came out. And frankly, the lone staff member in the gym—an associate warden—had a much bigger problem because he was essentially in the middle of the gym when the environment suddenly went south.

At this point the AW couldn't find a way out of the gym because he was literally smack-dab in the middle of a battle where steel is being slung all over the place. While the inmates were stabbing each other and committing every iota of their being to killing the dudes they were battling it out with, the AW was able to find a path to the correctional officers' office within the gym. Interestingly, he found the door unlocked, therefore unsecured and considered a serious security breach by the bureau. But it was a lucky break for the AW as he was able to quickly access a telephone and dial triple deuces. The AW urgently relayed a brief message indicating there was a shit storm in the gym and to lock the entire joint down until he and the staff could figure out what the hell had just happened.

The "why" part of this FUBAR (fucked up beyond all reason) would have to wait for now.

The two officers who were assigned to the Control Center quickly announced a recall over the penitentiary's loudspeaker while simultaneously activating the USP's siren, which in the event of serious incidents, alerts all Bureau of Prisons employees on the Lompoc federal reservation to drop whatever it is they're doing and report to the penitentiary for duty. It doesn't occur frequently, but when it does, it causes an immediate adrenaline rush. And the thing is, as I mentioned previously, in those days, that damn siren was going off way too frequently.

I always felt respect and admiration for my fellow Bureau of Prisons staff members across the way from my little, 1,500-bed low security facility. When you work at a minimum or low-level security facility, it's a rare occasion when you go home "late for quitting time," as we used to say. Conversely, USP Lompoc was one tough joint to work in. In those days, without an incredible amount of fortitude and resolve, a staff member would never survive "on the floor" with USP Lompoc's inmates.

As this shit storm in the gymnasium progressed, the AW quickly realizing the gym was "lost," ordered the crisis management crash cart, which included an L-8 multigrenade/projectile launcher, which looks like a short-barreled rifle with a giant rotating cylinder, like you would find on a common revolver, just much bigger. The L-8 multi-launcher, considered a "less-lethal" weapon, is capable of firing beanbags and other projectiles—including OC (oleoresin capsicum or pepper spray) to bring riotous situations under control. The specific color of the projectile is indicative of the strength of the charge that the operator is utilizing.

I think most folks would find this point about this particular disturbance interesting, but frankly, this is very much the rule and not the exception, and that is the fact that *not one* inmate laid a finger on the associate warden. And the reason for that is the inmates did not have a beef with the AW, nor any staff member for that matter; this was an internal issue connected to inmate "politics." As the AW had completed his call into the Control Center and was anxiously awaiting the crash cart, he noticed movement under the desk in the office; it was at that time he discovered the recreation specialist who had been assigned to supervise recreational activity in the gym and an inmate who wanted absolutely nothing to do with the intense raging that was occurring just outside the office door. Within minutes members of the facility's Special Operations Response Team

(SORT) and other staff arrived at the gym's main entrance and began to prepare for a dynamic entry into the gym to quell the mix of flying shanks, fists, and any other items that could be facilitated to harm another human being. Once the operations lieutenant arrived on scene, he assisted by preparing the L-8 for use, and once it was loaded, the AW ordered him to begin launching OC pepper spray into the cauldron of violence that had spread throughout the gym. When the lieutenant went to fire the L-8, it misfired. Although the gas was eventually "delivered" and dispersed, staff ended up having to fight many of the inmates that were involved; not because inmates had turned on staff, but because the inmates on both sides of the battle were so incredibly resolute about destroying the other faction, they could not be brought under control without the use of force. Once the situation was brought under control and the inmates were subdued and handcuffed, they were stripped out right on the spot. This action was not intended to humiliate or punish the inmates who were involved in the violence, but to ensure all weapons had been retrieved and secured to abate further bloodshed.

The facility ended up being in lockdown status for thirty days, which is an extraordinarily lengthy time to be down. Protracted lockdowns are stressful on staff and inmates, as nerves become frayed due to boredom, restricted and controlled inmate movement, and anxiety of further violence once the lockdown is lifted. In this case, however, I believe it was a good call to put the joint down for a month. The level and frequency of violence had been increasing at an alarming rate, and the leadership of the USP felt the only way to gain the attention, control, and compliance of the inmates was to remain in lockdown for an extended period. Plus, this gave time for investigators to determine what actually led to this event, therefore being able to identify and remove inmates attempting to agitate the situation. The specific cause of this event could have been a drug or gambling debt, issue of disrespect, or a host of other stupid things that higher security level inmates can get hung up on in their attempt to control "the yard" in terms of trafficking hard contraband that so many inmates seek in that type of environment.

* * *

Not to suggest that it can't happen, but it's quite rare anymore to have a correctional facility come unglued due to conditions of confinement, which was not uncommon in the seventies and before. Since the profession of corrections has increased—in terms of accountability, standardization, the implementation of inmate programs, attitude toward inmates, understanding cultural diversity issues, audits, accreditation, and training—the various causes are typically related to issues of contention between various inmate factions, gangs, and races, especially in higher security level environments.

With respect to disturbances, lockdowns, and riots occurring in American correctional facilities where the wheels come off, *almost* invariably you will find that a nexus exists between internal inmate issues and acts of violence, rather than being related to conditions of confinement or caused by an act of stupidity on the part of the facility's leadership and/or its staff. That's just the way it was during that particular period of time at the USP: Violent. Dangerous. Insane.

* * *

Since those days, however, the United States Penitentiary, Lompoc, was downgraded by the agency's leadership from a high security level facility to a medium security level institution, and although it still retains the name "USP Lompoc," in reality, it is a medium security level institution, thus making its mission similar to other medium security level Federal Correctional Institutions throughout the Bureau of Prisons. While the Bureau of Prisons was planning, constructing, and activating brand-new state-of-the-art penitentiaries at the time the new millennium rolled around, the original old school, hard-time penitentiaries of the agency, which included the United States Penitentiaries at Lompoc, Marion, Lewisburg, Atlanta, Terre Haute, and Leavenworth were monumentally difficult to maintain in terms of physical security upgrades and other appropriate modifications due to the age of the physical plant.

Consequently, over the years since that time, the missions of most of these old joints have been downgraded from high to medium security level. It made more sense to the agency's leadership to stop the bleeding by converting old school pens to medium security level facilities and building new penitentiaries, such as the United States Penitentiary, Canaan, Pennsylvania; and the United States Penitentiary, Hazleton, West Virginia, to name a couple.

* * *

I've stated on many occasions that the greatest failure of any correctional facility—and thus, the warden—is the escape of an inmate. And while it's unquestionably true that the escape of an inmate from secure custody is the greatest mission failure on the part of the facility, in reality, the *very worst* thing is the death of a staff member at the hands of an inmate(s).

I was extremely fortunate that in my twelve years as a warden to have never had a serious assault against, or the homicide of, a staff member. It is extremely rare that an inmate kills a federal officer (which all BOP staff are considered), especially in the Bureau of Prisons where there has been a total of twenty-six staff murdered in the line of duty, but the sad fact remains that it does occur. Other than the aforementioned case of USP Lompoc Officer Scott Williams, the "closest" I ever came to directly experiencing one of these tragedies—to be discussed later—was during my post-government career when I was working in the private sector in 2013.

THE UNITED STATES PENITENTIARY, CANAAN: ESTABLISHING THE CULTURE

From 2004 through 2007, I was the first warden to be assigned to the brand-new high security penitentiary known as the United States Penitentiary, Canaan, Pennsylvania. Canaan was my second assignment as warden, and I vastly cherished my time there. When I first arrived at Canaan in the spring of 2004 and drove around the facility, I was struck by how intimidating it appeared, with its rolls and rolls of concertina razor wire and immensely imposing grey cement structure. During those early days of my time at Canaan, long before we were fully staffed and had received our first inmate, I often wondered what the future would hold for the inside of this imposing prison. Many acts of serious violence had occurred in *all* of the agency's high security penitentiaries, and I knew Canaan would eventually be no different.

It was around this time that we received word on the outcome of a gruesome murder case that had occurred at the United States Penitentiary, Florence, Colorado. The information that was going around the agency was that two cousins were being housed in a Special Housing Unit cell at the penitentiary with one other inmate. Normally, BOP SHU cells are designed for two inmates, but due to population pressures in the Florence high security level prison, a third inmate had also been placed in the cell. At some point, staff observed a stream of blood running underneath the cell door and onto the range floor where these inmates were being housed. When staff investigated, it was readily obvious that they had a homicide on their hands because they could clearly see that one of the inmates had literally been gutted. Since it was abundantly clear that the one inmate was dead, staff began videotaping the scene and prepared to move the two living inmates out of the cell and process the crime scene.

Upon investigating how such a horrendous event could have transpired, staff discovered that the inmates were horseplaying initially, but eventually, an argument ensued then an assault and murder. Plus, alcohol was involved. It was learned the inmates had hoarded and hidden some oranges, allowed the fermentation process to occur, and had a high octane version of hooch. The inmate who had done the gutting said that he would not cooperate by coming out of the cell peacefully unless he could speak directly with the Special Housing Unit lieutenant. As staff continued to videotape, the assailant taunted staff and said that he had strung the victim inmate's intestines throughout the cell as a form of special decorations. As he sat on the body, speaking to staff, he smoked a cigarette and flicked the ashes into the cavity of the eviscerated body. At one point, he reached into the cavity, held the victim's heart up for all to see, and offered it to the lieutenant. While this degree of violence doesn't happen frequently, even in penitentiaries, it served as a stark reminder of the magnitude of responsibility that goes hand in hand with managing and leading a high security level correctional facility.

The very first day that I reported for duty at Canaan, there were a total of four staff members assigned to the facility that had reported for assignment ahead of me; they included two officers, one facilities type, and one warehouse officer. The interior of the facility had no infrastructure; there were no computers, no telephones, and no furniture. The first time I walked into my "office" and saw what I had to work with, which was nothing, I scrounged around the facility until I found a chair. I used a box as a desk. From that point, I assembled an executive staff team that, once approved by my regional director, and the rest of the agency's executive staff, filtered in over the next two to three months. Each of those folks had homes to sell, new schools to find for their kids, and a move from any number of states throughout the nation.

I had the extremely good fortune of having my entire executive staff approved by the agency. In reality, to have this occur was just shy of a miracle, as almost invariably there are political dynamics that come into play, and a warden may get one, some, or none of the folks that they request. In my case, I was incredibly lucky to get all of those seven or eight individuals whom I had requested. Suffice it to say that I had an absolute all-star executive staff during my tenure as warden at Canaan.

Perhaps the best training that I experienced throughout the course of my career occurred at Canaan shortly before the facility was dedicated, activated, and began receiving its first inmates. Somebody in the agency had come up with the idea to conduct annual Crisis Management Training (CMT) at USP Canaan, which at the time had been staffed up and ready to accept the first busloads of inmates but was still inmate-free. So, a plan was developed to send each of the region's nineteen facilities' Special Operations Response Teams, Disturbance Control Teams, Hostage Negotiations Teams, and Crisis Support Teams to our facility for a full week of crisis management training. It was an honor for my staff and me to host this training, which included hostage negotiations role-play, dynamic tactical assaults, and an assortment of other prison crisis-related training. The most interesting aspect of the training, because we had no inmates yet, was that staff were actually housed *inside* the facility for the entire week. All nineteen wardens, for example, resided in the facility's Special Housing Unit. Hell, I had my very own cell for that week…talk about experiencing the real thing for yourself! Obviously, we weren't locked in our respective cells, but it sure provided a very realistic account of what it was like for inmates to be in an SHU cell. Although some of my fellow wardens bitched about this decision, it made good sense, especially in cutting taxpayer costs for hotels, eating out, etc.

Four years after I had retired from government service, a horrible event unfolded at Canaan. On the night of February 25, 2013, inmate Jesse Con-ui viciously attacked thirty-four-year-old Officer

Eric Williams in a housing unit within the USP by repeatedly stabbing him. Con-ui—a known enforcer of the New Mexican Mafia prison gang—also slammed and stomped Officer Williams' head as he lay mortally wounded. It was determined that the coward Con-ui blindsided Officer Williams while he was walking the unit alone and unarmed. Con-ui knocked Officer Williams down a flight of stairs before stabbing and beating him. At the time of his attack on Officer Williams, Con-ui was serving an eleven-year sentence for drug trafficking. At this juncture in time, Con-ui can expect to serve the remainder of his sorry natural life in prison or be executed. Given the videotaped, physical, and eye-witness evidence again him, I can only hope for the latter.

As Bureau of Prisons practice dictates, Con-ui was transported to another high security penitentiary, the United States Penitentiary, Allenwood, Pennsylvania, shortly after he murdered Officer Williams. The reason for this is to ensure that legal justice is served. In reality, if an inmate who murders a staff member is left within the same facility, the chance of him being assaulted by staff is a legitimate concern. In these rarest of circumstances when a staff member is murdered by an inmate, the warden must quickly assemble a specialized team, typically select members of a Special Operations Response Team (SORT), which will be assigned the task of getting the inmate—who they all want to kill—safely moved from the facility where the assault took place, to another facility.

Staff homicides can occur in any correctional facility, but almost invariably occur in high security level penitentiaries, and other facilities—such as administrative level—where high security level inmates are incarcerated. In nearly all cases, those federal and other agencies (state, county, and local) where staff homicides have occurred at the hands of inmates, the staff victims served in the position of correctional officer. Furthermore, the vast majority of staff that are killed in the line of duty, are stabbed with homemade, sharpened weapons. In other words, shanks are typically used.

All of the staff killings that I have studied have had a substantial impact on me, and some have stayed with me more than others. One of those cases involved the homicide of a facilities (Mechanical

Service) foreman named Greg Gunter that occurred on Christmas Day, 1982, at the Federal Correctional Institution, Petersburg, Virginia. FCI Petersburg was not a penitentiary and never has been. As alluded to previously, the majority of prison violence occurs in higher security facilities, like penitentiaries, but it most definitely can occur in lower security level facilities.

There are so many unusual aspects to the senseless murder of Foreman Gunter that really hit me in the gut. On that fateful Christmas Day, Mr. Gunter was actually off duty and hunting with other off-duty staff members on the federal reservation of the facility. For safety reasons, these staff had facility-issued two-way radios on their person. When the radio traffic they were listening to indicated that an emergency was unfolding within the facility, Gunter and the rest of his hunting party selflessly responded to the prison without hesitation.

The radio traffic indicated a melee was in progress between Italian inmates from New York City and African American inmates from Washington, D.C., within the facility's chow hall, and things were quickly getting out of control, as the few staff that were present were unable to control or contain the escalating violence. However, due to the heroic efforts of the staff that were present in the chow hall, the fight was finally broken up. The DC inmates were contained in the dining hall while the Italian inmates were escorted out; this was accomplished in order to separate the two groups, which is standard protocol in this type of situation.

The DC inmates became more and more unruly and hostile as they were held in the dining hall, and eventually a window in the front of the hall was broken and inmates spilled unimpeded onto the institution's compound and began rioting. These inmates had armed themselves with anything they could find in the food services area, such as mop and broom handles, metal mixing paddles and blades, and other homemade and food service-related weapons. As the New York Italian inmates were being escorted, dozens of DC inmates, who were now armed with deadly weapons, mounted a full-scale assault on the New Yorkers. By this time, Foreman Gunter had entered the facility and went to the main compound where he found himself in the middle of the shit storm between the two inmate factions.

When Mr. Gunter attempted to stop the DC inmates from attacking the New York inmates, an inmate by the name of William Hackley hit him in the face with a huge commercial-style food service mixing paddle that severely injured the foreman. Once he was down on the ground, a multitude of other DC inmates viciously and repeatedly stabbed and beat Foreman Gunter. Although he was severely injured and completely prone on the ground, Hackley and another inmate continued the assault on Foreman Gunter by beating him with various pieces of metal while simultaneously stabbing him. It is one of the worst cases of an assault on a staff member, the details of which have always stayed in my mind. The most sickening aspects of this event for me is the fact that Greg Gunter was off-duty and enjoying Christmas Day and that he had a wife and two very young sons at the time of his murder. It's a horrifying event, but truly demonstrates the nature of BOP staff and their willingness to drop whatever they're doing at that particular time in order to assist their fellow staff.

* * *

Another example of the murder of a staff member at a bureau facility that was not a penitentiary is the February 5, 1983, murder of Correctional Officer Gary Rowe, at the administrative security level facility, the Metropolitan Correctional Center, San Diego, California.

In the evening hours of that Saturday, Officer Rowe became the victim of a botched escape attempt on the part of two inmates. Staff initially became suspicious when they noticed glass falling from above them from the facility's exterior. MCC San Diego, like most inner-city administrative federal jails, is a high-rise type facility. This prompted an inspection on the part of staff, including Officer Rowe and another correctional officer who was working on the same floor. The two officers split up in order to search separate wings of their assigned floor. Approximately twenty minutes later, the second officer found Officer Rowe, who had been pushed under a bunk bed.

Upon closer inspection, he saw that Officer Rowe was bleeding heavily from a severe head wound. Officer Rowe was rushed to the local hospital where, sadly, he died two days later. The after-action investigation revealed that Officer Rowe had caught an inmate in the act of breaking a window in order to facilitate an escape. Another inmate who was in the room with the inmate breaking the window, attacked Rowe from behind, repeatedly striking him in the head with a metal bar.

* * *

Another staff homicide that I typically referred to when training Canaan staff on safety and survival techniques occurred at a medium security level facility, the Federal Correctional Institution, Oxford, Wisconsin. Early on the morning of January 29, 1984, Correctional Officer Boyd Spikerman, was beaten and stabbed to death by at least two inmates. This staff homicide is so atypical, in that Officer Spikerman's murder was stupidly facilitated for the purpose of a few inmate "wannabees" who desired to be recognized and accepted by the Aryan Brotherhood.

The Aryan Brotherhood, like all prison gangs, takes their symbols—especially tattoos—*extremely* seriously. Not just anybody can "wear" one, and if that inmate has not been officially sanctioned as a blood-in blood-out member, simply by adorning an unsanctioned tattoo, is a potentially fatal act. If the offending inmate is *lucky*, he will be approached by a gang member, who will then question where and why he received a specific tattoo. If it is determined by the examining inmate the tat was not authorized, the offending inmate will be told that he is to immediately remove it by any means whatsoever. This is typically accomplished by burning the tat off or by "covering" it with another tattoo. If the inmate is not so lucky, he will be TOS, terminated on sight, by a gang member.

In the case of Officer Spikerman's murder, there were three inmates at Oxford who had had AB-related tats, such as a shamrock, or the initials "AB," tattooed on their bodies. However, as the investigation later revealed, the "approving" inmate who had "authorized" these three inmates to get these tattoo, was, in fact, not a legitimate gang member. This obviously created a dilemma for these inmates, so they came up with a plan, they believed, would curry favor with the ABs by killing a bureau staff member. Their plan, and how it unfolded, has always stayed in my mind and continues to give me a sickening feeling in my gut as I imagine what Boyd Spikerman went through on that cold January morning. Subsequent to arming themselves with shanks, one inmate crept into the unit office where Officer Spikerman was and, while the other two inmates kept watch, stabbed Spikerman. Although Officer Spikerman was severely wounded after he had been stabbed, he continued to show signs of life, so another inmate crushed his skull with a fire extinguisher. So senseless. So stupid. So sad.

* * *

During my tenure at FCI McKean, all of our staff were shocked by the senseless and horrible murder of Correctional Officer D'Antonio Washington when he was mortally wounded at the United States Penitentiary, Atlanta, Georgia, on December 21, 1994. On that morning in December, for no known reason, Officer Washington was assaulted by an inmate who was able to arm himself with a ball peen hammer. After knocking Officer Washington to the floor, the inmate continued to bludgeon him until he was nearly dead. Officer Washington succumbed to his injuries the next day on December 22.

* * *

The one and only female staff member killed in the line of duty within the Federal Bureau of Prisons was a lovely, blond-haired young lady named Janice Hylen. Miss Hylen, who was a contractual dietician with the bureau at the United States Penitentiary, Atlanta, Georgia, visited the high security penitentiary on November 21, 1979. She was there to assist with the special diet meal planning of inmates. An inmate named Robert Hogan walked past the room that

Miss Hylen was working in at the time and could see that she was alone. Hogan attacked, raped, and then beat Miss Hylen to death. Hogan admitted at one point to investigators that it had always been his intent to kill a female staff member, and he was simply looking for an opportunity to do so. Later, after Hogan had eventually been moved to the United States Penitentiary, Marion, Illinois, he was murdered by another inmate. Poetic justice.

* * *

I've studied all of the murders of BOP staff in the line of duty, as well as staff killed in other correctional systems, and while each is horrendously unique in its own way, some cases have really stuck with me. That is certainly true in the case of young Jose Rivera, a correctional officer at the United States Penitentiary, Atwater, California, that occurred on the afternoon of June 20, 2008.

As Officer Rivera was attempting to place two inmates into their cell, both began viciously assaulting Officer Rivera by stabbing him with shanks. As Officer Rivera retreated, he fell down, and the two inmates pounced and continued stabbing him until he died. The most tragic thing about this senseless murder was the fact that Officer Rivera was only twenty-two years old; he was a navy veteran, including two tours in Iraq, and he had been with the bureau for ten months. It's just enough to make you sick.

* * *

I was also extremely fortunate to have never worked at a correctional facility—at least during my time there—when an escape of an inmate was experienced. As I've mentioned previously, an escape from secure custody is an abysmal failure on the part of the facility in question. It is humiliating, embarrassing, and in *every* case, the result of staff complacency, apathy, corruption, or what we commonly referred to as "shortcutting." The bottom line, if all staff conscientiously carry out their assigned duties and responsibilities, it is damn near impossible for an escape to occur. Unfortunately, however, we know that human nature dictates otherwise, and there will inevitably be times when staff let their guard down, take shortcuts, or in some cases, become corrupt. When any of these "enemies" of sound correctional management occur, it's just a matter of time until something bad happens. It's the role of the warden and his or her executive staff, department heads, and other supervisors to ensure staff are on their game, day in and day out. It's absolutely imperative.

In studying the nuances of prison and jail escapes, at least 99 out of a 100 times, one can point to that act of shortcutting, which often times was exacerbated by other dynamics, and say, "Yep, here's where staff screwed up. No wonder they had an escape." I've studied dozens and dozens of inmate escapes from secure custody, and a few of them have made quite the impression:

* * *

In December 2012, two inmates escaped from the Metropolitan Correctional Center, Chicago, Illinois, in a most brazen manner. The two inmates apparently had collected and hid numerous bedsheets until they felt they possessed enough to scale the federal high rise jail, that is, if they were lucky enough to get on the outside of the facility.

Cellmates Jose Banks and Kenneth Conley were able to secure tool-like instruments and eventually chiseled away at their extremely narrow cell window until there was an opening big enough for them to squeeze through and reach the outer wall of the facility. The ongoing hammering the two inmates engaged in was not heard by staff because of noisy construction that was simultaneously occurring in the jail at that time. The fact of the matter is, once the inmates had defeated and removed their cell window, they found themselves dangling *seventeen stories* above downtown Chicago. Somehow, they made their way down the bedsheet "rope" they had fashioned and onto a parking garage before they scampered away. Although Banks and Conley did not kill anybody once they had escaped and were eventually recaptured, the fact that an escape had occurred from a secure facility was totally unacceptable. The investigation that ensued demonstrated that cell shakedowns (searches) were not being

conducted in a thorough and consistent manner as policy, procedure, and practice dictate. Had staff been diligent in the performance
of their duties, it is more than likely this escape would have been
thwarted.

* * *

Right around the time that my staff and I were activating the
new United States Penitentiary, Canaan, on April 5, 2006, a convicted murderer named Richard McNair escaped from the high security facility of the United States Penitentiary, Pollock, Louisiana. This
was a wake-up call for my staff and me as we were stunned to hear
how the ingenious McNair pulled off the near impossible.

All able-bodied inmates in the Bureau of Prisons are required to
have a job in the facility where they are being housed. McNair's job at
USP Pollock was that of a factory worker. The factory shipped manufactured goods out of the facility on a routine basis, so that in and
of itself leaves a facility vulnerable to escape unless strictly followed
protocols are in place. For example, when a loaded trailer leaves a
secure facility, it is thoroughly inspected inside and out before being
parked in a secure vehicular sally port, which is isolated from pris-
oner access. A vehicle sally port is essentially big enough for a fairly
large trailer to be parked in and surrounded by double fences and
ringed with concertina razor wire. Once a vehicle is parked in the
sally port, a number of inmate counts must be conducted, typically
five throughout a full twenty-four-hour day and cleared before that
trailer can be hooked-up to a truck and can leave the facility. This
was not the case in the escape of McNair. McNair, for all intents and
purposes, shipped himself out of the facility with the assistance of
unknowing staff.

On that April day in 2006, McNair constructed an extremely
small space for his contorted body to barely fit underneath piles of
mailbags that would be shipped out of the facility on a pallet. Once
the bags were stacked on the pallets, they were shrink-wrapped and
moved. McNair, after fashioning a breathing tube, pulled as many
mailbags as he could on top of himself so that he would remain hid-

den. Sometime around 10:00 a.m., the pallet that contained McNair was shrink-wrapped and moved to a warehouse outside the secure perimeter. Had staff strictly followed protocol by moving the pallet onto a trailer, then immediately moving it into the vehicular sally port to sit through various inmate counts, the escape would have been thwarted. The shrink-wrapped pallet that McNair was concealed in, however, was moved from inside the secure perimeter to a warehouse outside the double fences and concertina razor wire. McNair, under the concealment of the pallet of mailbags, had just shipped himself out of the facility.

McNair, a convicted murder, had already escaped from two other non-bureau correctional facilities, so it was quite natural that the BOP's leadership freaked out when he escaped from Pollock. McNair is the only inmate that I'm aware of who has facilitated successful escapes from a local correctional facility, a state facility, and a federal high secure level penitentiary. With escapes in the Federal Bureau of Prisons from secure custody being so rare, this one was even worse because this dude was seriously dangerous and had somehow escaped from one of the BOP's high security level penitentiaries. That is *extremely* rare. In fact, no inmate had escaped from secure custody in the entire Bureau of Prisons since 1991. It was thought that McNair had to have had assistance from other inmates, but later said he had acted alone and the investigation was unable to prove otherwise.

Once McNair found himself shipped outside of the facility and worked his way out of his ingenious hiding spot, he eventually began jogging down a railroad track that was nearby the facility. He was wearing a white T-shirt and gray gym shorts, so he looked like a regular dude that was out for a jog. While jogging on the railroad tracks, McNair was stopped and challenged by a local police officer, the entire encounter of which was taped by the officer's patrol dashboard camera. When McNair was unable to produce identification, the officer asked him what his name was and where he was from.

McNair told the local officer he was from a town nearby the facility and provided the name of Robert Jones. The officer and McNair talked and joked around, and the officer laughingly said that

McNair actually fit the description of a convict who had recently escaped from Pollock penitentiary. From the encounter, you would have thought the two were just shooting the shit on a pretty spring day, as it was remarkable how calm, cool, and collected McNair remained while, simultaneously, the officer was clearly unprepared to actually believe that McNair was the convicted killer that everybody and their brother in local law enforcement and corrections were desperately seeking. In fairness to the officer, the photo on the flyer that the facility provided to local law enforcement was not an accurate representation of how McNair appeared on that day.

When the police officer again asked McNair what his name was a few minutes after asking him the first time, McNair said he was Jimmy Jones. So while McNair was damn good in being convincing, he slipped up by giving the cop two different first names, but the officer never picked up on this fact. Within a few minutes, the officer told McNair that he could be on his way, and he most certainly was because he was not recaptured until October 2007, long after he had made the US Marshals Service 15 Most Wanted list and had been featured on the television show *America's Most Wanted*. As one might imagine, McNair was transferred to and, to the best of my knowledge, is still incarcerated at the bureau's super max, the ADX in Florence, Colorado.

* * *

One of the craziest escape attempts in the course of my career occurred in the early 1990s at the Federal Correctional Institution, Phoenix, Arizona. There were two inmates at FCI Phoenix, a medium security level facility that were able, somehow, to have wire cutters and two .9mm pistols mailed into the factory's warehouse where they worked. As they attempted to breach the facility's secure perimeter, they were encountered by the roving perimeter mobile patrol correctional officer assigned to that post. A firefight ensued whereby one inmate was shot and killed, and eventually, the other inmate committed suicide by shooting himself.

* * *

When I first entered onto duty with the Federal Bureau of Prisons, we were schooled about an escape that occurred sometime in the 1980s at the United States Penitentiary, Leavenworth, Kansas, that has always served as a teaching point. While there have been all kinds of audacious and crazy escape attempts throughout the history of American correctional facilities, the fact of the matter is that most attempted escapes are facilitated in much less dramatic fashion. Specifically, that would be accomplished by simply walking out the front door of the facility. Why not go out the easy way rather than risk being shredded to pieces on the perimeter fence or shot down by a correctional officer in the tower?

The inmate at Leavenworth had slowly and methodically accumulated staff and civilian clothing over a period of many months. If an officer inadvertently left a BOP jacket in the visiting room, this inmate would latch on to and hide it. Over time, he was able to accumulate an agency windbreaker, a maroon tie that BOP staff wore back in the day, a BOP hat, and other pieces of clothing that certainly made him, when fully dressed out, appear more like a civilian or staff member than an inmate. Once this guy had a full set of clothing and was also able to secure a clipboard, he was prepared to put his plan into action.

On the day he decided to go for it, this particular inmate got dressed in his "costume" and made his way through the secure checkpoints located throughout the joint. He had posed himself as a safety inspector of some sort from the community and had finished his "work" for the day. Long story short, he simply walked right out the front door of the facility. We were told that he was captured a short time later, but the fact that he was able to just *walk out* of the facility had to be one hell of an eye-opener. This is why correctional leaders constantly educate staff on the importance of not leaving clothing items anywhere in the facility unsecured because if so, it's guaranteed it will find its way into the possession of some creative-minded inmate. Interestingly enough, the same type of thing occurred at FCI Lompoc around 1990 when an inmate was able to somehow walk right out the front door of the facility.

* * *

This also brings up the point of how important it is for control room officers to positively identify *every* staff member entering and leaving the facility. Anytime new staff are hired, a photograph of each is immediately placed in control for the purpose of positive identification until the control room officers can identify them by face and name. It is furthermore imperative that all staff engage in the same practice. Anytime I was leaving the facility and other staff were with me in the sally port, if I didn't positively recognize each of them, I would politely ask for their identification. It's just not something you can take a chance on. Along the same lines, every BOP facility has a "look-alike" file that's maintained in the Correctional Services (captain and lieutenants) office. The look-alike file contains photographs of inmates who look like a certain staff member. You'd be surprised how closely some staff members resemble a particular inmate; it's uncanny and also a serious threat to the security of the facility if you're not on top of the issue. The same look alike file is maintained in the control center as well so that control room officers are aware if there is an inmate in the facility who looks like a staff member.

* * *

For the safety, security, and general accountability of staff in the facility, every correctional facility should also have a "chit board." A chit board is a rudimentary but effective method for knowing what staff members are inside the facility at any given time. The chit board, quite simply, is a large square board attached to a wall located near the entrance leading into the secure portion of the facility. The chit board will have pegs with a chit on each peg; each peg/chit represents a staff member. Say my peg is number 1. When I enter into the sally port, I turn the chit from OUT to IN because I'm entering the facility, and anybody who glances at the chit board will quickly be able to discern that I am inside the secure facility. When I leave work, I simply turn the chit over from IN to OUT. Chit boards are so important because when there is an institution emergency, say a hostage situation, it is imperative that staff quickly determine if every staff member inside the secure facility has been accounted for.

BROOKNAM AND THE BIG APPLE

Throughout my career, like almost all senior bureau staff, I moved whenever and wherever the agency wanted me to. It's just the way it was, not only in terms of enhancing one's upward mobility, but we were all conditioned to be loyal to the agency, and that meant sacrificing for the good of the agency. In retrospect, it seems a bit foolish to have disrupted the lives of my family and uprooting them at the whim of the bureau, but that is in fact how it was, and I suppose it's no different now for those who want to move up into leadership positions. Throughout my government career, I always said that I would go anywhere the agency wanted me to go, as long as it was not New York City. That meant, quite possibly, Yankton, South Dakota; Milan, Michigan; Pekin, Illinois; and a bunch of other rural and urban bureau institutions located throughout this vast country. But I always said there was *no way* that I would drag my family to the Big Apple, *especially* not to the Metropolitan Detention Center, Brooklyn, New York.

The Federal Bureau of Prisons has two facilities in New York City: MDC Brooklyn, and the Metropolitan Correctional Center, New York. Both are federal jails, in that the vast majority of both facilities' population is comprised of pretrial/presentence inmates. MCC New York is located in lower Manhattan, while the MDC Brooklyn is located on west side of the New York harbor.

I was the warden of the United States Penitentiary, Canaan, when I received a call from my boss, the Northeast Region's regional director. He shocked me by saying the agency's executive staff wanted me to transfer to Brooklyn, and it was important to them that I do so. Wow. My first thought was, "Not only no, but *hell* no!" When I

129

expressed to my boss that a move to Brooklyn was not exactly at the top of my preference profile, he worked on me until I agreed to run it by my real boss, my wife. In short, we discussed it and decided, what the hell, let's go do it and enjoy the unique culture and everything else that New York City has to offer. For a bumpkin from West by God Virginia, this was most definitely going to be a culture shock!

* * *

Serving as the warden of the Metropolitan Detention Center, Brooklyn, New York, was the most challenging assignment of my career. Before going any further, it's important to adequately convey my feeling with respect to the "MDC," as most folks refer to it. The fact of the matter is the *vast majority* of Brooklyn's staff are highly dedicated correctional professionals who simply do their jobs in an honest and professional manner. I developed a strong bond with the incredibly dynamic and diverse staff there. What makes working at this facility so difficult are the few turds that give all the other staff a bad name and perpetuate the stereotype that correctional workers are a bunch of knuckle-dragging incompetent brutes.

The Metropolitan Detention Center consists of two high-rise buildings (east and west), about nine stories in height that are connected by an underground tunnel. The east side building is ancient, as it was constructed just prior to 1920, and was not acquired by the agency until 1992. The west side building was "added" adjacent to the east side and activated in 2000. The two towers, in total, can house approximately three thousand inmates with a square footage total of over half a million feet. Our staffing compliment was right around 550 positions, but only around 500 of those positions were encumbered throughout my time there.

MDC Brooklyn is a very large and incredibly dynamic facility. Given its mission as a "jail," inmate turnover and movement into and out of the facility is nonstop, every day. Because Bureau of Prisons jails are administrative security level facilities, every kind of inmate comes into that facility. There are minimum, low, medium, and high security level inmates in Brooklyn. Once their case is adjudicated, some of the inmates might spend a year in prison, conversely, there are those who will score out as a high security level, maximum custody inmates, and those individuals will likely be incarcerated for the rest of their lives. You see those that are drug addicted and going through withdrawal, you see the mentally ill, you see violent drug dealing killers, dirty cops, terrorists, organized crime types, and everything else in between. It is, in fact, one hell of a unique joint.

In those days, the MDC was considered the most "troubled" facility throughout the entire agency, and I believe it is viewed no differently today. There were many facilities, to include all of the agency's high security penitentiaries, that experienced more violence, but Brooklyn was a much different animal. The underlying problem at Brooklyn, as it had been for quite a few years, was the pervasiveness of staff corruption.

Given the bureau's obsession for correctional professionalism, sometime during the early days of my career, the agency instituted a policy regarding staff rules and expectations, referred to as the agency's Code of Conduct. By that time, especially with the "war on drugs," the agency was growing exponentially. Within a decade, the agency had nearly quadrupled in terms of inmates, facilities, and staff. Consequently, it was becoming more and more difficult to achieve consistency and control in terms of how wardens were handling and adjudicating staff misconduct. The problem was you could have a warden in one region who would fire a staff member for an act of misconduct, yet a warden operating within another region might issue a one day suspension without pay for the very same act. As one can imagine, the agency's union for correctional officers soon realized they could appeal and get certain disciplinary actions against staff overturned due to the inconsistent nature of applying discipline. So the bottom line was to achieve consistency while improving the overall professionalism of the agency.

As part of the Bureau of Prisons' new Code of Conduct, wardens were compelled to report *all* allegations of misconduct, regardless of their severity, and *all staff* were required to report every potential act of misconduct up through their chain of command. If, during the course of an investigation into staff misconduct it became known that a staff member had knowledge of that alleged act of misconduct but failed to report it, he or she would also have a referral made against them for failing to report an act of misconduct. Suffice it to say that we wardens spent an inordinate amount of our time dealing with personnel issues and this issue was exponentially exacerbated at the Metropolitan Detention Center, Brooklyn.

* * *

Once an allegation of staff misconduct reaches the desk of the warden, he or she is mandated to report the allegation, and a case file is opened. Many allegations were extremely minor in nature and/or known to be pure bullshit; nevertheless, each and every allegation had to be reported to the agency's headquarters at the Central Office in Washington, D.C. The way the process worked was once the allegation made its way through the facility's chain of command, the warden sent a fax referral to the Office of Internal Affairs in Washington. If there was any potential for the act of misconduct to be criminal in nature, OIA referred the case onto the US Department of Justice's Office of the Inspector General. If the OIG deemed that the allegation could be classified as criminal in nature, or if they simply wanted to be involved due to the severity of it, everything was put on hold until OIG decided to come to the facility and initiate the investigation.

What typically happened with most cases, however, was once OIG kicked the referral back to the Bureau of Prisons—because it was not criminal in nature—the case could then be handled by the BOP. At that point, the referral was kicked back to the facility's warden for investigation at the local level, or the Office of Internal Affairs could decide to conduct the investigation itself. This typically occurred in instances of allegations that were serious in nature, yet administrative, rather than criminal.

To frame some perspective regarding the degree of misconduct that was occurring those days at the Metropolitan Detention Center, Brooklyn, one only had to look at the statistics. Prior to being assigned to Brooklyn, I had been the warden at USP Canaan and FCI Lompoc. While I was at Lompoc, the highest number of open cases of alleged staff misconduct that we had was about fifteen. This included all allegations of misconduct, including everything from failing to report for duty on time to passing contraband to an inmate. On average, we had about the same number of open cases during my tenure as warden at Canaan, yet at Brooklyn, we consistently maintained two to three hundred open cases at any time, and during our peak of open cases, we actually had over four hundred unresolved cases. This statistic is a bit misleading because the majority of these cases was minor in nature, such as being late for work, but on the other hand, we had plenty of serious allegations—some criminal in nature—that we were constantly dealing with.

As I've stated before, from my perspective the Federal Bureau of Prisons is the most professional, credentialed, correctional agency in the county, if not the world. Think how often you hear something in the media about the bureau. It very rarely happens because the agency is loaded with capable, competent, well-trained staff, who are consummate correctional professionals. Yet there was Brooklyn, and the agency's leadership had grown weary of the steady stream of staff corruption there. My executive staff and I lovingly referred to the joint as "Brook-nam," rather than Brooklyn because most of the time the frenetic pace of the facility seemed very Vietnam-like to us.

Even with its less-than-stellar-reputation, at the time I arrived at Brooklyn in 2007, the facility had recently experienced some very high-profile staff corruption cases, which only darkened the cloud that hung over the facility. The "hottest" MDC, Brooklyn staff corruption case that was being bantered about in the New York City newspapers in 2008 was the case of the captain, or "chief of the guard" as they would say in the old days.

* * *

In November 2002, the captain of the MDC was one of the most visible and respected members of the entire staff. Next only to the associate wardens and the warden, the captain is typically the highest-ranking member on staff. In fact, oftentimes captains are viewed by staff as the *most* powerful staff member within the facility. This is due to perceived personality traits, experience (especially in penitentiaries), and the fact that captains, at least the effective ones, are on the compound rather than stuck in some office. What made this case of staff corruption so painful for the agency was the fact that the captain at the MDC was one of those captains: he was out and about, dynamic, and had the respect of many who worked for him.

Unfortunately, on that day in November, the captain and an associate warden were making their rounds throughout the facility's Special Housing Unit. It was in the SHU that the captain saw an inmate, who was locked inside his cell, with a T-shirt wrapped around his head. The captain appropriately told the inmate to lose the shirt in order for staff to have complete visibility of the inmate. The inmate essentially said "fuck you" by refusing the captain's order to remove the shirt from his head. The captain and the AW then left the SHU.

About half an hour later, without the associate warden in tow, the captain returned to the Special Housing Unit and had a lieutenant and two correctional officers follow him to the inmate's cell who had his "dreads" wrapped in the T-shirt. Once these staff were standing outside the locked cell of the inmate, the captain made a decision to violate one of the most basic security tenets in any special housing unit, and that was to unlock the cell with the inmate inside *and* not handcuffed. The captain then made the dangerous decision to enter the cell. Up to this point, bureau policy had been severely and foolishly breached, but things were about to become criminal.

As soon as the cell door was popped, the captain and his staff entered the cell and a fight immediately erupted. As the fists flew, the captain and one of the officers slammed the inmate to the ground and handcuffed him. The captain reportedly then took the inmate's sheet from his bed and fashioned it to appear like a noose. He then told the staff who were assisting him that their "story" would be the inmate was attempting to kill himself by hanging, and they had no choice but to breach the cell. The degree of violence was such that photographs later showed some of the inmate's dreadlocks and blood on the floor of the cell. At this point, policy, procedure, and practice had been severely breached, the inmate had been assaulted, and now there was a conspiracy to cover up what actually occurred in that cell. In 2008, during my tenure as warden at Brooklyn, this case was finally adjudicated, with the outcome of all these staff losing their jobs and being convicted of felonious charges at the federal level.

* * *

Another hot staff corruption case at MDC Brooklyn occurred in April 2006 within an elevator used to transport inmates throughout the facility. On that particular day, a correctional officer activated his body alarm, summoning help because of an altercation with an inmate whereby the officer was slightly injured. Once the inmate was subdued and handcuffed, he was transported to the Special Housing Unit by three correctional officers on the elevator. All Brooklyn staff are well aware that hundreds of cameras are located throughout the facility, to include the elevators. Taping occurs 24/7 for obvious reasons to include potential staff misconduct and criminal behavior. For a number of days, it was known that the camera in the elevator was not functioning, thus staff believed their actions were not being taped. But unbeknownst to them, a technician had recently repaired the camera, and it was functioning as designed. Well, these three officers were highly pissed that this piece of shit inmate had injured one of their cohorts, and he simply wasn't going to get away with that without a little bit of payback. Big mistake. Once the elevator door closed, one of the officers tripped the handcuffed inmate and threw him down. Once the inmate was down, another officer, performed a tap dance on the inmate's neck and shoulders while his two buddies watched. The three staff then proceeded to cover the whole incident up and got their stories straight. Another conspiracy. The technician staff member who had repaired the camera happened to stumble upon the footage of what occurred in the elevator and brought it to the attention of the facility's executive staff. From that point, an investigation ensued. Of course, the staff involved maintained that the inmate had attacked them, but the tape obviously proved otherwise. Again, three careers trashed, and they went from the position of federal officer to federally convicted felon.

* * *

It's difficult to adequately convey just how much time my executive staff and I spent dealing with staff misconduct. It seemed that we saw everything there was to see in terms of crazy staff issues and behavior. Every day was an adventure. We had this physician that worked at Brooklyn who was extremely eccentric. This dude oftentimes wore the same clothes over and over, always looked disheveled, and apparently shaved with his eyes closed, because he had a mustache on one side of his face but not the other. On top of all his idiosyncrasies, he was uncomfortable with inmates and socially inept. One day we had to perform a forced cell move on a female inmate who was having a mental health breakdown. This particular inmate needed to be moved because she had smeared her own excrement all over the cell that she was in. Once the team was suited up and we went through the policy requirement of videotaped confrontation avoidance, the team entered the cell, easily pinned her down, got handcuffs and leg-irons on her, and moved her to another cell. As policy requires, a medical professional—typically a physician's assistance—must then perform a medical examination of the inmate to determine and document any injuries, abnormalities, etc. In this case, we actually used the doctor for the exam because no other certified medical staff was available at the time.

Once our female inmate was calmer and the doctor initiated the medical exam, all seemed to be going as planned when, suddenly, the inmate exploded with rage and aggression and "trapped" the doctor's head between her legs. Although there were five correctional officers there to assist, this inmate locked the doc's head between her legs with such force that it took what seemed forever to extricate the poor doctor. I happened to be present while this was unfolding, observing the forced cell move. The inmate saw me while she had the doctor's head between her legs and looked at me like she was possessed. She then screamed, "Warden! How would you like to smell my pussy?!!"

136

Suffice it to say, I quickly removed myself from the area; it was just another day at Brooklyn.

* * *

The rectal cavity is the most effective and common location where inmates "hide" serious contraband simply because nobody wants to look there and, frankly, minus cause to do so, other than departing from or arriving at a facility, looking up an inmate's back-side isn't routinely done.

On another occasion at MDC Brooklyn, my staff told me they were absolutely certain there was a gang leader that was communicating with the outside world via a cell phone. We conducted search after search with no results; we simply couldn't locate his phone. At some point, we decided to obtain regional office authorization to conduct an x-ray of this inmate. Lo and behold, he had a cell phone and a Bluetooth attachment, all nicely wrapped up in cellophane and, yes, stuffed up inside his pooper. The joke was we always wondered if the inmate preferred having his phone in vibrate mode.

* * *

There was an incident when a probationary correctional officer was being screened into the facility when the lieutenant who was performing the screen noticed what appeared to be a handgun in the officer's purse. When the lieutenant asked the officer to empty her purse, a .9mm pistol rolled out onto the x-ray machine belt. She was immediately sent home and placed on suspension pending an investigation; later, her employment was terminated for attempting to introduce a weapon into the facility. She was lucky to have only been fired rather than prosecuted. When asked what she was thinking by bringing a gun into the facility, she said that she had been threatened by some of the inmates on the unit where she was assigned. Rather than bringing that to the attention of the facility's leadership, she decided to handle the matter herself by bringing a gun into the facility. Brilliant.

* * *

Our staff noticed the distinct smell of feces in a particular area of an inmate dorm that shouldn't have been there. Upon searching the unit, it was discovered an inmate had a couple dozen pellets that were coated in a thin rubber and in the approximate shape and size of a Robin's egg. This inmate had been busted at LaGuardia Airport for attempting to smuggle heroin into the States from a South American county. Drug agents seized everything that he had concealed on his person but failed to determine what was inside of his body via x-ray. Once our staff found the pellets of heroin hidden inside his mattress, he revealed that he had swallowed them then passed them the following day.

* * *

One day my office was contacted by the United States Attorney's Office from the Eastern District of New York, which is located in Brooklyn. The request was to assist other federal law enforcement organizations in escorting an unnamed billionaire drug kingpin from Columbia who was scheduled to fly into JFK Airport under "heavy escort" then transported to the MDC. Obviously, we agreed, and one of my associate wardens and I made the trip late one afternoon to JFK. Once we arrived and were escorted to a Command Center at the airport, we were briefed on who was coming in and what the plan would be for getting him to our jail. Around 6:00 p.m., the inmate's flight had landed, and he was quickly packed into a cruiser. With approximately a dozen cruisers from a variety of law enforcement agencies, this individual was rushed, lights and siren, from the airport in Queens to the MDC in Brooklyn. The feds were taking no chances with this guy, who had the means and resources to mount an escape attempt. While he was being rushed to the jail, snipers had set up at various strategic points around the outside of the facility. It simply wasn't the sort of thing you see every day in the profession of corrections, but this was Brooklyn.

* * *

We had another correctional officer who experienced a mental breakdown of some sort while working in one of the facility's units. According to inmates in the unit, the officer began acting extremely strange by babbling incoherently. Later in the shift, the officer became catatonic-like, sitting at her desk and staring straight ahead, refusing or unable to speak or perform her duties. To seek staff assistance, an inmate actually picked up the officer's phone and dialed triple deuces. I know that it's happened before, but that was the one and only time in my career where an *inmate*, rather than a staff member, dialed triple deuces.

* * *

One day at the MDC, the front lobby officer called my secretary to inform me that an NYPD officer was in the front lobby and was requesting to see me. As I meandered downstairs, I couldn't imagine why NYPD wanted to speak with me, especially with no advance warning. Waiting in the lobby was a traffic officer from the largest police department in the United States—about 32,000 sworn officers at that time—who said he had something he wanted to show me, but I would have to go outside to his cruiser to see what he was talking about.

The officer had a tape-recorded event that he wanted me to see, which involved a traffic stop he had made on one of our correctional officers. As I sat in the traffic officer's cruiser and watched the tape, I felt extremely embarrassed and humiliated. The idiot correctional officer, who had a string of sustained incidents of misconduct against his record, immediately began giving the police officer a ration of shit the very moment he was pulled over for excessive speed. The correctional officer told the cop that he was a "federal law enforcement officer," and he would see to it that the cop was appropriately reprimanded for screwing with his day. It got to the point where the cop was ready to call for backup and arrest the correctional officer because he was being such an asshole. In reality, BOP staff are not permitted, according to the Code of Conduct, to attempt to influence an officer of the law when stopped for a traffic offense or any other time for that matter. The bottom line was the correctional officer had yet another internal affairs case opened against him for this incident which eventually led to his dismissal.

* * *

MDC Brooklyn, like most other federal correctional facilities, typically houses a small group of minimum security level inmates who assist with the day-to-day tasks of maintaining the grounds on the outside of the facility. I received an allegation one morning indicating that one of our mechanical services employees was allowing an inmate to work on her vehicle. This, clearly, is a violation of the Code of Conduct and obviously highly unprofessional and inappropriate. As we investigated the matter, we discovered that while the inmate mechanic was working on the staff member's vehicle, another employee served as a "jigger," which meant he was watching the area for other staff who might walk into the area. When this happened, he would signal the inmate and other staff member to stop working on the vehicle and act as though legitimate work was being performed in the parking lot. Although this is relatively minor in the overall scheme of staff misconduct, it was just more bullshit that had to be dealt with. It meant another referral to the Office of Internal Affairs, another full-scale administrative investigation, and another misconduct statistic at Brooklyn.

* * *

One afternoon we experienced a serious security breach that could have been disastrous, but we were lucky. The control center officers *always* have an obligation to ensure they know precisely who they let out of the facility and who they let *in*. On this particular day, the officer "working" the security doors in the Control Center popped the door for somebody he thought was a staff member. The individual was then permitted to pass through at least three secure checkpoints as the officer continued to open doors from his post in the control center. The individual who proceeded to walk into the "secure" bowels of the facility was, in fact, a defense attorney rather than a staff member. Another referral to Office of Internal Affairs!

* * *

Early one day just before our daily morning meeting began, the captain and the associate warden over Correctional Services told my secretary that it was important that they see me at once. Not good. Once inside my office and the door closed, they proceeded to tell me how an inmate was placed in restraints all night without food, water, and from what they knew, had not been appropriately counted during scheduled inmate counts throughout the night. This may not sound like such a big deal, but it is, especially when you and your staff are responsible for the well-being of every inmate under your care, contol and custody. As usual, this was another OIA referral, investigation, and disciplinary case against the shift lieutenant, who was the individual responsible for ensuring this type of thing does not occur on his shift.

* * *

We received a complaint that one of our supervisors in our business office had allegedly been sexually harassing some of our female staff members. During the course of the investigation into this allegation, we discovered that the supervisor had been making what the complainants said he referred to as a "gold offer" of $500 to any of the attractive female staff if they would only go out with him. Only at Brooklyn!

* * *

During my tenure at Brooklyn, two prominent New York Police Department detectives, sadly, became inmates at the facility. Louis Eppolito and Stephen Caracappa were alleged to have been working on behalf of the New York area mafia Lucchese crime family. Caracappa had been a member of the Organized Crime Homicide Unit in Brooklyn, and it was alleged that the two detectives received hundreds of thousands of dollars from the mob to inform, kidnap, and murder certain individuals that the mob wanted gone. Both detectives were eventually convicted on a string of federal offenses, including but not limited to extortion, obstruction of justice, murder, and conspiracy to commit murder. During my time at Brooklyn, both of these inmates were the quintessential polite and cooperative inmates; however, both were convicted and sentenced to life in prison.

* * *

One of the more intriguing cases that occurred during my tenure at Brooklyn, was the arrival of inmate Aafia Siddiqui, a Pakistani native who had completed a bachelor degree at MIT and later a PhD at Brandeis University. I had received a call from my boss, the Northeast Regional Director, informing me that we would be receiving a hard-core al-Qaeda terrorist who had attempted to kill FBI personnel and United States military staff in Ghazni, Afghanistan. When Siddiqui was delivered and admitted into the detention center, I was rather shocked to see a diminutive, quiet female who appeared to be scared to death, and in obvious pain, as she was recovering from being shot in the torso. But then again, appearances are sometimes misleading.

Siddiqui, who had been known as the "Daughter of the Nation" in Pakistan, did not make eye contact with staff and said as little as possible, and her arrest had been viewed in her home country as an attack on Muslims and the religion of Islam. According to what little information we had received on Siddiqui when we accepted her, she had completed the requirements of a PhD in 2001 and had returned to her native Pakistan. We were also told that high-ranking al Qaeda operative, Khalid Sheikh Muhammad, had revealed during his multiple interrogations that Siddiqui was a courier for al Qaeda; therefore, she was wanted by the FBI for questioning. A few years later, in 2008, Siddiqui was arrested by authorities in Ghazni, Afghanistan. When taken into custody, Siddiqui was found to have in her possession poison and instructions for bomb making. The day after being taken into custody in Afghanistan, Siddiqui was apparently left unrestrained and unattended for a short time. Unfortunately, one of her interrogators had left his rifle on the floor. Showing her true colors, Siddiqui picked up the rifle and began shooting at the Americans. Fire was returned, and Siddiqui was shot in the gut. Although she received immediate medical attention, she later alleged that she was raped and tortured by representatives of the United States.

As I said, Siddiqui was extremely quiet and rarely spoke until she was compelled to appear in court. On the day that she was to be transported to federal court, Siddiqui was ordered—like all prisoners—to submit to a strip search in the presence of a female correctional officer. Siddiqui suddenly became belligerent and extremely verbally abusive, refusing to submit to the strip search. We initiated our confrontation avoidance protocols and politely informed her—while being videotaped—that the strip search was a matter of bureau policy and procedure that all inmates coming into or exiting the facility have to submit to. This simply enraged Siddiqui as she screamed at the top of her lungs that this was nothing more than a Jewish conspiracy and that we, "American devils," were part of the Zionist regime that controlled and dictated the actions of the American government. I mean she just came unglued, but eventually, she understood that we meant business and eventually relented to the strip search when confronted with the reality that she would be forced, physically, if necessary, if she did not comply with staff orders.

By the time her case was adjudicated in February 2010, Siddiqui was convicted of armed assault, attempted murder, using a firearm, and assault. After she was found guilty, as usual, she blamed the Jews. In the end, she was sentenced to eighty-six years in prison. If you ever get a chance to study the trial proceedings in this matter, it is, at least in my opinion, one of the more interesting cases out there. Siddiqui is scheduled for release in 2083.

* * *

If you've ever wondered why strip searches are invariably performed on inmates leaving and entering a correctional facility, this example illustrates why it is so important. One day in 2008, the United States Marshal Service buses were loaded with inmates en route to the United States District Court for the Eastern District of New York (Brooklyn) and the United States District Court for the Southern District of New York (Manhattan). Before boarding the buses or vans, all inmates are strip-searched and placed in restraints by Federal Bureau of Prisons Receiving and Discharge staff and, once loaded in the vehicles, become the responsibility of the USMS.

It was business as usual once the buses arrived at their destinations and inmates shuffled into holding areas within the courthouses. On this particular day, one inmate sat quietly as his case proceeded through the arraignment process. The prosecuting official in this matter was an assistant United States attorney, known as AUSAs. As the female AUSA was addressing the court, the inmate in question suddenly and without warning leapt from where he was seated, and although he was partially restrained, was somehow able to rush the AUSA and attempted to stab her with a small shank. While extremely rare, this can obviously happen. The AUSA was, understandably, extremely shaken yet uninjured as USMS court staff quickly reacted and slammed the inmate to the floor. It was all over in a flash but was just the beginning of the finger pointing to follow.

As I received information about the attempted assault and the video of the event was reviewed by me and my team, as expected, I received a call from the chief deputy of the USMS for the Eastern District. Of course, he wanted to know how this inmate could have manufactured and concealed a deadly weapon and wanted to know how in the hell our staff could have allowed it to happen. The fact of the matter was nobody but the inmate knew where the weapon had come from or how it was obtained, which he refused to divulge.

As I pointed out to the chief, the weapon could have been obtained on his bus, or it could have come from the MDC, but the fact was, nobody knew or could prove either theory. Frankly, I was a bit defensive about the incident because throughout my assignment at Brooklyn, our staff were looked down on by other members of the federal law enforcement family. Of course, this was due to the dirty staff the local community and members of law enforcement were always hearing about. I certainly understood the sentiment, but it was nevertheless unfair.

* * *

One of the biggest clusters that the administrative staff at Brooklyn has to contend with is the staff housing, known as Dayton Manor, which is located a few miles from the facility. Dayton Manor, situated in Brooklyn a few blocks from the US Army base, Fort Hamilton, is a huge apartment building that's owned by the federal government. Dayton Manor permits staff from Brooklyn and the Metropolitan Correctional Center, New York, to reside there at a slightly discounted rate relative to community rental rates. Because New York City is such a high cost of living area, many staff—especially those who are transient—choose to live there. The managing oversight falls to the warden at Brooklyn, thus exacerbating the multitude of issues that must be dealt with.

Dayton Manor issues were discussed at our morning meetings with the same degree of inmate and staff issues that arose within the facility. Because there were literally hundreds of staff and their families residing at Dayton Manor, we had all the drama that went with a small community. Complaints of domestic disputes, affairs, noise, and intoxication were commonplace, and we had to deal with each and every one of them.

Because Dayton Manor was what it was, it was imperative that we had at least one facilities staff member on the premises for the purpose of making repairs involving heating, ventilation, air-conditioning, etc. One day we received a complaint from one of our officers who had recently been promoted and was in the process of moving to another facility, that much of her property—especially her electronic devices—were missing. After an investigation ensued, it was discovered that our facility worker had "removed" the items for "safekeeping." Bullshit. He had stolen them from the officer and was dealt with appropriately.

* * *

One day we had four or five inmates who began arguing in one of Brooklyn's housing units. Suddenly things became violent as they broke into fighting. It was one hell of a fight but did not involve weapons. Staff responded and eventually brought the fight under control. As standard protocol dictates, we had tape pulled to analyze how and why things went down. Once we started looking at the tape of the fight, we could see staff responding to these inmates who were knocking the heck out of each other, but we noticed that there was one correctional officer who was actually running the *other* way. Turned out that this officer was always bragging about his black belt status in karate and what a tough guy he was. The fact was, when the shit was going down, he pussed out and went the other way.

* * *

There was so much drama that occurred on a daily basis at Brooklyn, it simply became the norm. We had a few correctional officers who were hitting on inmate visitors; this becomes a threat to the general security of the facility because an inmate could very well put a visitor up to seducing and compromising a staff member in order to manipulate him or her into bringing contraband into the facility or facilitating an escape.

* * *

We had an officer, who we could never catch, that we knew was smuggling in pornographic tapes for inmates. We had another officer, who after being pulled over by the New York Police Department for a traffic violation, actually called 911 to report that the officer had no right to detain him because he was a federal officer. We had one officer who had intercepted two letters that an inmate was mailing; one letter was for his wife and the other letter was for his girlfriend. The officer deliberately switched the letters with the envelopes so that the letter intended for the girlfriend went to the wife and the letter intended for the wife went to the girlfriend. These issues of constant consternation became very frustrating for my team and me because the behavior of these idiots, and the media attention they garnered, represented a tiny fraction of the professional and hardworking staff at Brooklyn, but these folks made it appear that our staff, as a whole, was a group of knuckle-dragging sadistic buffoons.

* * *

We had an inmate threaten to file an administrative remedy (grievance) because his penis continued to get infected. It was the inmate's contention that the government was obligated to circumcise his penis because of the supposed repeated infections. We had another inmate who jumped from a second floor tier landing because he felt he was "obligated to die." Fortunately, he was not killed and, luckily, received only moderate injuries.

We had one of the Somalia pirates who was involved in the infamous attack and hostage-taking on the ship MV *Maersk Alabama*. In April 2009, the siege was ended after a tactical assault by US Special Forces (Navy SEALS). Of the four pirates who attacked the Maersk, this dude was the only one that wasn't taken out by our military. One of the interesting things I recall about this idiot was that he allegedly did not know how old he was, so a dental exam was performed in order to make an estimation with respect to his age.

* * *

We had a female correctional officer, who, after becoming familiar with an inmate, quickly fell in love with this guy, and once the inmate had satisfied his sentence and was released from the facility, she eventually decided she wanted to make a life with him and move into his place of residence. You already know this scenario is not going to end well. The ex-girlfriend of this inmate, who still held a flame for him, follows him one day through the streets of Brooklyn. The bonded-out inmate went to the MDC and parked across the street from the facility while the "ex" surreptitiously observed him from a safe distance. Eventually, the girlfriend observed the inmate get into a vehicle belonging to the female correctional officer. The girlfriend then calls United States Probation and reports that a MDC correctional officer is living with a former inmate. Naturally, the United States Probation Office folks follow up because they now have the ex-inmate on supervised release, which is another term for probation, and there is a host of stipulations that must be met by the inmate in order to avoid being violated and returned to prison. When the probation officer entered the residence and began to question things, the correctional officer tried to bullshit the probation officer by saying she was a federal law enforcement official. Not only does the bureau's Code of Conduct prohibit fraternization with inmates and ex-inmates, but the probation officer sees drugs in plain sight. Needless to say, the former inmate's term of supervised release (probation) was violated and he returned to incarceration, and the correctional officer was terminated. Rather than dealing with the internal issues inherent to managing and leading a correctional facility, my team and I were constantly devoting inordinate time to dealing with staff drama and violations of the Code of Conduct. Later, it was determined that the same correctional officer had been having a relationship that we believed to be sexual in nature, but could never prove, with a death penalty–eligible inmate. It was, after all, Brooklyn.

* * *

One day, a female inmate reported that she had been "raped" by a male correctional officer. We initiated an investigation, eventually involving the FBI and the Office of the Inspector General. It was eventually uncovered that the correctional officer had been having sexual intercourse with the female inmate, which he said was consensual. In short, it is my belief that the female inmate—along with another female inmate—had lured the correctional officer into thinking that he could have "consensual" sex (of course, there is no such thing between ward and warder) with these two inmates and all was good. Not so much. After our dirty CO had some fun with the inmates, they reported it and backed up their allegations with plenty of facts that were irrefutable. The end result was termination and prosecution for the staff member and civil litigation by the inmates against the government.

* * *

You see all kinds of bizarre things relevant to sex and sexuality in correctional facilities. We had a correctional officer at Brooklyn, who became "friendly" with a male inmate, but to what degree, we weren't sure until an investigation uncovered the fact that she had taken photographs of her genitalia with a cell phone and then sent them to an inmate. Of course, when confronted, she resigned.

* * *

Another time we had a correctional officer who was heavily involved with the facility's employees' Special Emphasis Program, which was designed to educate staff on the importance of staff cultural diversity and understanding. This individual was extremely self-righteous and frequently asked to speak at general staff meetings to "educate" staff on her special program goals. One day an inmate reported to us that he had been having sexual activity with this same correctional officer. Naturally, we reported the allegation to the appropriate chain of command and an investigation ensued. When the correctional officer adamantly refuted the allegation to investigators, she was told that the inmate could identify a tattoo that was on her rear-end and had some sex tapes of them doing their thing. That was the end of the interview. The staff member resigned on the spot.

We later discovered that she had introduced drugs and cell phones to this inmate for months.

* * *

MDC Brooklyn became very personal for me in December 2008 when, a few days before Christmas, an anonymous call was placed to the main phone number of the facility that was received in our control center. The caller told the officer who fielded the call that an individual who was a member of a New York City mafia crime family who was currently being housed at the MDC—along with help from individuals on the outside of the facility—was planning to kill me. The information was immediately sent through our chain of command and reached me within minutes of the call. One of my associate wardens immediately suggested that we lockdown the facility, but I refused that notion because I was concerned that locking down the jail would make me look weak and scared, the latter of which was not far from being accurate. After sending the information through the chain of command above me, the threat was passed along to the FBI and an investigation ensued immediately. I give a great deal of credit to special agents of the FBI because they were all over this matter within the same day while the reaction within my agency was quite opposite. I was offered protective services that more than likely would have been provided by the US Marshals Service, and while I turned down this suggestion, I found it quite telling when I failed to receive even one phone call from my superiors expressing concern. When the FBI interviewed me, I expressed suspicion the call may have been initiated by an inmate who was being housed in our Special Housing Unit and was currently under the most restrictive guidelines imposed by the US Department of Justice and the Federal Bureau of Prisons. This, however, was not the case. The US Attorney's Office in the Eastern District of New York served a subpoena for incoming calls to the MDC during the time the threatening call was received, and the FBI determined the call to the control center had been made from a nonworking phone number at Saint Francis Hospital.

I watched my back to and from work every day very carefully and constantly worried about my family; it's not every day that one receives an anonymous threat indicating a New York mob family wants to rub you out, but in the end, it appeared to the FBI—and I concurred—the phone call was made in an attempt to manipulate actions on the part of me and my administrative staff. It was determined that one crime family was attempting to ruin the holiday season for another crime family member by giving the impression the call was legitimate when, in fact, by all appearances, the call was intended to manipulate us into placing the inmate in our Special Housing Unit. In short, one crime family was screwing with another crime family at my expense. It turned out to be nothing at all, but it sure as hell had me on edge for more than a month while the investigation was conducted and concluded.

* * *

I suppose some things never change. Within two weeks of the time of this writing, a correctional officer and two correctional supervisors—lieutenants—were charged with various civil rights violations of female inmates at the MDC. Specifically, these individuals, who swore an oath to uphold the constitution and protect inmates, were charged with sexual abuse, aggravated sexual abuse, and a variety of other crimes that deal with alleged sexual activity between them and inmates. The United States Attorney's Office for the Eastern District of New York (Brooklyn) alleges rape, threats, and intimidation of these staff against female inmates. If true, this is very sad indeed, and as I have stated before, it will bring another black eye to the Bureau of Prisons, the MDC, and the hard working and dedicated majority of the staff that are employed there.

LIFE AFTER THE BUREAU
OF PRISONS

After nearly three years of constant drama at the Brooklyn facility, living on an Army Base, Fort Hamilton, and dealing with the inherent pressures of living in the city, I was ready to try something different. While I could have remained another seven years with the agency, I was being heavily recruited by a company in private corrections and had decided to retire on my first day of eligibility, which was my fiftieth birthday. Working at MDC Brooklyn and living in New York City was an enriching experience for me and my family, but it was time to go, so I made my retirement effective and moved to State College, Pennsylvania, in the fall of 2009.

I immediately began employment with a private corrections company at a low security level facility in rural central Pennsylvania that was contracted by the Bureau of Prisons to house criminal aliens. The typical inmate of the 1,500 or so that we housed was a convicted felon stemming from charges in the United States, coupled with being in the country illegally. Subsequent to serving their court-imposed sentence, the vast majority of these inmates would be subsequently deported to the country of their origin.

Working in private corrections was an interesting life experience, and at the time, I thought it would be a good thing. "Private prisons" are for-profit entities where inmates are incarcerated by a third party (a company) that is contracted by the government (which could be a county, state, or in my case, the federal government). If these inmates were being locked up by the government, so what if they were being outsourced to private companies to incarcerate them?

I had a very decent federal law enforcement retirement, now coupled with a nice salary, and stock options. Made sense to me. What I had failed to grasp at the time, however, is the fact that these companies, as *all* companies, are driven by one thing: money. I quickly discovered that as long as the facility remained secure, and no major incidents occurred, such as escapes, homicides, and suicides, the singular goal is profit. When shit storms occur, however, say an escape for example, it brings heavy scrutiny from the government, which leads to action by the company because their contract is then threatened.

Since everything is driven by profit in the world of private corrections, the goal is to ensure that one's key indicators were where they needed to be. Key indicators include escapes, escape attempts, homicides, suicides, assaults with and without weapons, positive urine tests, rate of staff misconduct, inmate administrative remedies, audit results, staff turnover, sexual assaults, inmate incident reports, security breaches, policy deficiencies, and others. All of these items are monitored very closely by the government and the company and are indicative of how well or poorly the facility is operating. Screw up as the warden in the government, and although you'll more than likely lose your wardenship and be moved into some much less visible job, you'll still retain your pay. Screw up in the private industry and your ass is gone. I was lucky to have had extremely good staff at the Pennsylvania facility, and we were considered operationally outstanding. There was almost no drama whatsoever at this facility. We had approximately one fistfight per month and, frankly, the operational aspect of the prison was simple. Going from MDC Brooklyn, where we had two to three thousand inmates and five hundred staff (not to mention the incredible high level of drama), to a sleepy low security level prison of 1,500 inmates and about 200 staff was a real break in the action. But it was a miserable situation for me because many of our officers were spoiled, although they were earning around $23 per hour, working in an environment where almost nothing happened, and had what I saw as excellent benefits.

The only serious event that occurred in my near three years there was the assault of one inmate against another utilizing scalding water. One inmate got pissed off at another inmate, so he boiled water in the microwave and then threw it on the other dude, causing significant injury. Other than that, my job revolved around keeping the Bureau of Prisons' contract monitoring oversight staff happy while simultaneously jumping through company hoops to ensure profits were maximized. Even though I was soured by the constant bitching of the union, I had a group of outstanding department heads and executive staff that I was very fond of, and we developed some unique programs designed to avoid threats to the key indicators of the facility. One of the coolest things that we implemented was the utilization of complacency exercises. Complacency exercises were developed with the aim of keeping staff on their toes by being cognizant of routine avoidance and bad habits that invariably lead to correctional facility disasters. For example, we would take an inmate and deliberately place him in an area of the facility where clearly he didn't belong and had no business being there. Then, from a concealed location, we would monitor the actions of staff to see if and when they determined the inmate to be out of bounds and if they would take appropriate action. We conducted these exercises monthly with the goal of improving the overall safety and security of the facility.

* * *

I lasted nearly three years at this prison before finally deciding it was time to really retire, so I gave notice and gave it up. I hung out at the house for a while but quickly became bored and decided to get back in the game one more time when I was recruited by another company to serve as the warden of a large privatized county jail near Philadelphia, and it turned out to be quite the experience.

* * *

The Philadelphia area jail was super interesting as much as it was dynamic, as thousands of inmates were processed into and out of the facility each year. It was there that the magnitude of the opiate crisis hit me, as we constantly saw severely addicted inmates come into the jail and engage is desperate behavior to gain access to heroin and/or other opiates to stave off the torturous symptoms inherent to drug withdrawal. It was also at this facility where I realized that our nation's jails had essentially become, unfortunately, the replacement for mental health facilities, many of which had closed between the 1960s and 1990s. Those individuals who are seriously mentally ill, especially those with no family and financial support who end up on the streets, eventually find their way into their local jails. The national disaster that is currently the opioid crisis was just coming to the forefront and simply exacerbated the situation of correctional facilities serving the additional role as mental health centers. Talk about an eye-opener.

* * *

We experienced more than our fair share of harden criminals at this jail. We received a thirty-eight-year-old man who was a fourth-degree black belt in karate, and the legal guardian of his six-year-old nephew. The uncle was preparing the little guy for bed when, according to his version of things, the youngster became "uncooperative." He therefore proceeded to beat this poor little kid for forty-five minutes with a belt, then a second heavier gauge belt when he perceived the first belt was not having its intended consequences. Subsequent to the beating, this poor excuse of a human being poured peroxide on the boy's wounds and sent him to bed naked. When the uncle checked on the kid later, he discovered him unresponsive with a brown liquid seeping from his mouth. He took the kid to the hospital where the little one was pronounced dead.

* * *

Another jail case involved a twenty-two-year-old mother who testified that on Christmas night she was abducted by three thugs while she was smoking a cigarette and looking at her phone in the parking lot of a tavern. The assailants, who eventually landed in our facility, wore ski masks, approached the victim with guns, forced her into the passenger seat of her car, and drove to a secluded area.

Although she was gagging and vomiting, all three forced her to perform oral sex. Then, the victim was forced onto her stomach and raped. The entire ordeal lasted five hours.

* * *

During two years at this facility, I witnessed numerous inmates spread their own excrement all over their bodies and the insides of their cells. Those suffering from schizophrenia and other forms of severe mental illness are more apt to engage in this type of behavior, but the most difficult, yet sane, inmates who will do anything to disrupt the smooth operation of a correctional facility will engage in this type of behavior too. When inmates fill a cup with their own feces and urine, the "cocktail," is, quite naturally, frightening for staff, not only because it's incredibly repugnant, but more so because there is the fear of contracting hepatitis C and a host of other serious diseases or illnesses. There was one female at the jail who was mentally ill and refused to take medication; consequently, when "happy," she danced in her cell continuously and I mean literally for hours. However, when she was "unhappy," she constantly raised hell and spread crap all over herself and the cell walls and windows. It was awful, and every time I toured the medical unit where she was being housed, I could tell by the smell—or lack thereof—whether she was happy or unhappy long before I actually could see her.

* * *

We received a gay female pediatrician who had been living with another woman at the time. Each woman had adopted the other's biological child during the time they were together and shared custody of their children. Estranged from each other at the time of this event, the partner of the pediatrician reported to police that she had driven to the pediatrician's house with both children in her vehicle. The purpose of the visit was to drop the doctor's child off to her. When the little girl exited the vehicle, an argument ensued. The doctor then slapped her partner and suddenly produced a gun and began firing wildly. The victim's car had three bullets shot through the windshield, and she was struck as well. The remaining child in the vehicle was uninjured, but the partner suffered gunshot wounds to the face and torso.

* * *

We had another thirty-two-year-old man who, we had been told, had suffered from mental illness for a number of years. This individual went to his mother's house and asked for money. When the mom declined, the son said that "something bad" was going to happen at her sister's house, yet when the man left, the mom failed to warn the sister of what had just transpired. A few hours later, when the sister arrived at her home, she was surprised to find her nephew in her kitchen. The mentally ill individual then stabbed his aunt. When she collapsed on the floor, a cousin of the assailant walked in and she was also attacked by being slashed in the arm and pushed down a set of stairs. At that point, the uncle of the assailant walked in and saw what was going on. He screamed at the attacker to put down the knife, which the assailant eventually complied with and the police were summoned. I actually got to know this inmate fairly well as he always wanted to speak with me during my rounds throughout the facility. Invariably, he told me that he wanted to be my "friend." In reality, as we learned from his family, this individual really wasn't a bad guy, but he was lower-functioning and was seriously mentally ill but refused to take his medication. Consequently, like so many of these individuals, he ended up harming someone and landed in a correctional facility.

* * *

The most unusual, insane thing that occurred in my time at the Philadelphia area jail, and perhaps throughout my entire career, dealt with a female inmate, who was seriously opioid addicted and extremely emaciated. This individual was being held in a medical cell while being managed for withdrawal and detoxification protocol. She said she was on the toilet because she thought she "had to poop" when, suddenly, she delivered a baby right in the damn toilet. She began to scream for assistance, and one of our registered nurses, who happened to be in close proximity ran into the cell and rescued a relatively healthy baby from drowning in the toilet. According to the inmate, she had "no idea" that she was pregnant. I don't know what the outcome of the baby's ultimate destination was, but she would have to be detoxed herself before going on to live a normal life. The joke inside the jail after this occurred was whether the facility's count would be plus one once the baby was born. It was the only time in my entire career that I have ever known a baby to be born in a jail toilet, and I certainly hope it's the last.

* * *

Being a large, metropolitan area jail, our staff not only saw a huge influx of addicted and mentally ill inmates, but some extremely dangerous individuals as well. Being a jail rather than a prison, we housed inmates of all security levels, and I experienced working with some of the most dangerous individuals of my career there. We had one inmate, who appeared to be mentally unstable to say the least, who was facing charges for killing his baby who was seven months old. Although the police had yet to locate the baby's body, it was believed that to spite the baby's mother, he had tossed the baby off of an unknown bridge or killed and buried the baby in an unknown location. He had said he despised the baby and repeatedly told the mother that he wanted it dead while bragging that he could get away with murder. At the time of this writing, he is charged with murder, kidnapping, and abuse of a corpse, but his case has yet to be adjudicated.

EPILOGUE

When I retired as a practitioner from the profession of corrections in 2014, I began a new journey as a jail and prison expert witness in the field of civil litigation. Over the course of the last four years, I have had the unique opportunity of contracting with two State Attorney General Offices and another state's protection and advocacy department. These days, my goal is to improve the overall profession of corrections. I have assisted defense teams in the representation of correctional public entities, and I have likewise assisted in the representation of inmate plaintiff teams. How I decide if I will accept a case as an expert in civil litigation hinges on a very simple principle: can I get behind the case and support it wholeheartedly? As I told my staff many times over the years, be objective and simply call balls and strikes.

Have no doubt, if we are to evolve as a society and a race of human beings, it is imperative to improve our correctional systems in this great nation of ours. Jails, prisons, and detention facilities will, someday or another, eventually release about 95 percent of the 1.2 million or so individuals who are currently incarcerated in the United States. We have to ask ourselves, given the fact that the vast majority of those currently incarcerated will eventually return to our communities, do we not have a moral, ethical, and legal obligation to do everything in our power to return these people no less angry and violent at the end of their sentences, compared to what they were when they entered the criminal justice system? I would submit that it is imperative that we do, and we must continue to explore methods for improving the overall profession of corrections.

ABOUT THE AUTHOR

 Cameron K. Lindsay was born and raised in Morgantown, West Virginia. He has worked in the criminal justice field virtually all of his adult life as a police dispatcher, police officer, criminal justice college instructor, and twenty-eight years in corrections. Cam worked in correctional facilities of all security levels, and for twelve years served as the warden of three prisons (two federal, one privatized) and two jails (one federal, one county privatized). Cam earned a BS degree from Fairmont State College, and MA and MS degrees from West Virginia University. He now works as an expert witness in matters of civil litigation relevant to corrections. Cam and his wife, Deanna, reside in Morgantown.